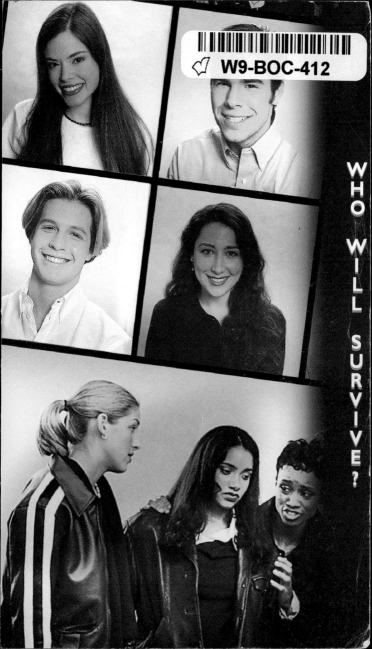

WHO WILL SURVIVE?

IT'S GOING
TO BE A
KILLER
YEAR!

Is the senior class at Shadyside High doomed? That's the prediction Trisha Conrad makes at her summer party—and it looks as if she may be right. Spend a year with the FEAR STREET seniors, as each month in this new 12-book series brings horror after horror. Will anyone reach graduation day alive?

Only R.L. Stine knows...

Trisha Conrad

LIKES:
Shopping in the mall my dad owns, giving fabulous parties, Gary Fresno

REMEMBERS:
The murder game, the senior table at Pete's Pizza

HATES:
Rich girl jokes, bad karma, overalls

QUOTE:
"What you don't know will hurt you."

Clark Dickson

LIKES:
Debra Lake, poetry, painting

REMEMBERS:
Trisha's party, the first time I saw Debra

HATES:
Nicknames, dentists, garlic pizza, tans

QUOTE:
"Fangs for the memories."

Jennifer Fear

LIKES:
Basketball, antique jewelry, cool music

REMEMBERS:
The doom spell, senior cut day, hanging with Trisha and Josie

HATES:
The way people are afraid of the Fears, pierced eyebrows

QUOTE:
"There's nothing to fear but fear itself."

Jade Feldman

LIKES:
Cheerleading, expensive clothes, working out

REMEMBERS:
Ice cream and gab fests with Dana

HATES:
Cheerleading captains, ghosts, SAT prep courses

QUOTE:
"You get what you pay for."

Gary Fresno

LIKES:
Hanging out by the bleachers, art class, gym

REMEMBERS:
Cruisin' down Division Street with the guys, that special night with that special person (you know who you are...)

HATES:
My beat-up Civic, working after school everyday, cops

QUOTE:
"Don't judge a book by its cover."

Kenny Klein

LIKES:
Jade Feldman, chemistry, Latin, baseball

REMEMBERS:
The first time I beat Marla Newman in a debate, Junior Prom with Jade

HATES:
Nine-year-olds who like to torture camp counselors, cafeteria food

QUOTE:
"Look before you leap."

Debra Lake

LIKES:
Sensitive guys, tennis, Clark's poems

REMEMBERS:
Basketball games, when Clark painted my portrait

HATES:
Possessive boyfriends and jealous girlfriends

QUOTE:
"I would do anything for you, but I won't do that."

Stacy Malcolm

LIKES:
Sports, funky hats, shopping

REMEMBERS:
Running laps with Mary, stuffing our faces at Pete's, Mr. Morley and Rob

HATES:
Psycho killers, stealing boyfriends

QUOTE:
"College, here I come!"

Josh Maxwell

LIKES:
Debra Lake, Debra Lake, Debra Lake

REMEMBERS:
Hanging out at the old mill, senior camp-out, Coach's pep talks

HATES:
Funeral homes, driving my parents' car, tomato juice

QUOTE:
"Sometimes you don't realize the truth until it bites you right on the neck."

Josie Maxwell

LIKES:
Black clothes, black nail polish, black lipstick, photography

REMEMBERS:
Trisha's first senior party, the memorial wall

HATES:
Algebra, evil spirits (including Marla Newman), being compared to my stepbrother Josh

QUOTE:
"The past isn't always the past—sometimes it's the future."

Mickey Myers

LIKES:
Jammin' with the band, partying, hot girls

REMEMBERS:
Swimming in Fear Lake, the storm, my first gig at the Underground

HATES:
Dweebs, studying, girls who diet, station wagons

QUOTE:
"Shadyside High rules!"

Marla Newman

LIKES:
Writing, cool clothes, being a redhead

REMEMBERS:
Yearbook deadlines, competing with Kenny Klein, when Josie put a spell on me (ha ha)

HATES:
Girls who wear all black, guys with long hair, the dark arts

QUOTE:
"The power is divided when the circle is not round."

Mary O'Connor

LIKES:
Running, ripped jeans, hair spray

REMEMBERS:
Not being invited to Trisha's party, rat poison

HATES:
Social studies, rich girls, cliques

QUOTE:
"Just say no."

Dana Palmer

LIKES:
Boys, boys, boys, cheerleading, short skirts

REMEMBERS:
Senior camp-out with Mickey, Homecoming, the back seat

HATES:
Private cheerleading performances, fire batons, sharing clothes

QUOTE:
"The bad twin always wins!"

Deirdre Palmer

LIKES:
Mysterious guys, sharing clothes, old movies

REMEMBERS:
The cabin in the Fear Street woods, sleepovers at Jen's

HATES:
Being a "good girl," sweat socks

QUOTE:
"What you see isn't always what you get."

Will Reynolds

LIKES:
The Turner family, playing guitar, clubbing

REMEMBERS:
The first time Clarissa saw me without my dreads, our booth at Pete's

HATES:
Lite FM, the clinic, lilacs

QUOTE:
"I get knocked down, but I get up again…"

Ty Sullivan

LIKES:
Cheerleaders, waitresses, Fears, psychics, brains, football

REMEMBERS:
The graveyard with you know who, Kenny Klein's lucky shot

HATES:
Painting fences, Valentine's Day

QUOTE:
"The more the merrier."

Clarissa Turner

LIKES:
Art, music, talking on the phone

REMEMBERS:
Shopping with Debra, my first day back to school, eating pizza with Will

HATES:
Mira Block

QUOTE:
"Real friendship never dies."

Matty Winger

LIKES:
Computers, video games, Star Trek

REMEMBERS:
The murder game—good one Trisha

HATES:
People who can't take a joke, finding Clark's cape with Josh

QUOTE:
"Don't worry, be happy."

Phoebe Yamura

LIKES:
Cheerleading, gymnastics, big crowds

REMEMBERS:
That awesome game against Waynesbridge, senior trip,
tailgate parties

HATES:
When people don't give it their all, liars, vans

QUOTE:
"Today is the first day of the rest of our lives."

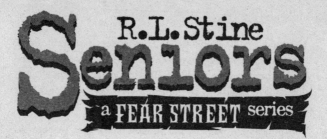

R.L. Stine

Seniors
a FEAR STREET series

episode four **No Answer**

A Parachute Press Book

A GOLD KEY PAPERBACK
Golden Books Publishing Company, Inc.
New York

Check out the new FEAR STREET® Website
http://www.fearstreet.com

A Gold Key Paperback Original

Golden Books Publishing Company, Inc.
888 Seventh Avenue
New York, NY 10106

FEAR STREET and associated characters, slogans and logos are trademarks and/or registered trademarks of Parachute Press, Inc. Based on the FEAR STREET book series by R.L. Stine. All rights reserved, including the right to reproduce this book or portions thereof in any form whatsoever. For information address Golden Books.

Copyright © 1998 by Parachute Press, Inc.

GOLD KEY and design are registered trademarks of Golden Books Publishing Company, Inc.

ISBN: 0-307-24708-2

First Gold Key paperback printing October 1998

10 9 8 7 6 5 4 3 2 1

Photographer: Jimmy Levin

Printed in the U.S.A.

No Answer

Prologue

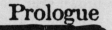

Clarissa Turner stared at the bouquet of lilacs in her hand. Stared into the purple petals, losing herself in their brilliant color.

The car passed through the massive iron gates of Shadyside Memorial Cemetery and stopped.

"It's time, Clarissa," her mother said gently.

Clarissa took a deep breath. She brushed her long curly dark hair back behind her ears and climbed out of her seat.

Her mother put an arm on her shoulder. "I'm proud of you, Clarissa. I'm glad you're finally able to come out here to see your sister."

The air felt chilly against Clarissa's warm

1

brown skin. No sun. Just thick gray clouds. Yellowed leaves blew across the dry grass of the cemetery. The gravestones looked so cold.

Dead leaves . . . dead grass . . . dead people.

I don't want to remember Justine this way, Clarissa thought. I want to remember her laughing . . . shopping at the Division Street Mall . . . our long talks . . .

"Are you okay?" her father asked.

Clarissa tried to smile, but her mouth wouldn't work right. "Yeah," she replied softly. "No problem, Dad."

Clarissa's father led the way through row after row of graves. "Here she is," he finally declared, pointing to a small granite headstone underneath a withering tree.

Clarissa froze. This was the moment of truth. And she *wasn't* ready. She wanted to run. Run right out of Shadyside Memorial Cemetery.

But I have to show everyone I'm okay, she thought.

Dr. Sayles. Her parents. They all said that this was the next step for her. To see her sister's grave.

Clarissa leaned over and read the marker.

JUSTINE TURNER—BELOVED DAUGHTER AND SISTER.

She drew a deep breath. Her eyes began to sting with tears. Some of the lilac stems crumpled in her fingers, and Clarissa realized how hard she was holding them.

"Why don't you give her the flowers," her father suggested, his voice gentle.

She nodded stiffly and set them down next to the gravestone. "Justine and her lilacs," her mother murmured, shaking her head. "They were just about her favorite thing in the whole world."

"I hate them now," Clarissa whispered. "They remind me of her funeral."

She squeezed her eyes shut and tried to picture the night her older sister died.

Nothing. A total blank.

Why couldn't Clarissa remember? All those tests . . . all that time in Dr. Sayles's clinic . . . all the discussions.

Clarissa's parents told her that she was the one who found Justine's body. That Justine tripped and fell down the stairs while she was talking on her cordless phone.

The fall broke her neck.

Less than two months ago. An eternity.

What a stupid way to die, Clarissa thought angrily. What a waste. But it was still so hard for her to believe that Justine was really gone. Forever.

That's why she had to spend those weeks in Dr. Sayles's clinic. Accepting it. Coming to terms with it.

Now Clarissa was out. This was her first day of freedom.

And it was time to say goodbye to Justine. Time to begin her life again. Go back to Shadyside High. Be a senior.

Clarissa shuddered, holding her jacket close against the cold fingers of the wind. "I miss her," she whispered.

"I know, honey," her mother replied softly. "We all do."

Chapter One

"You're back!" Debra Lake ran down the front steps of Shadyside High and gave Clarissa a hug. "You're really back!"

Clarissa couldn't help grinning. "Hey, girl!" she said as they marched up the steps and through the doors of the school. The front hall was crowded with kids. Clarissa's stomach fluttered with excitement.

And a little fear.

What were people saying about her—after being in the clinic? "Everyone must think I'm nuts," she muttered.

Debra wrinkled her nose. "Are you *kidding*? Everyone is so psyched to see you, Clar."

Clarissa forced a smile.

5

"Will you *relax*?" Debra told her. "Everyone is jealous that you got some time off."

Clarissa let out a breath of relief. "Thanks, Deb."

"Hey, what are friends for?"

"So what have I missed?" Clarissa asked, glancing around the crowded hallway. Stacy Malcolm and Mary O'Connor rushed past her. Dana Palmer and Marla Newman stood by a row of lockers, laughing.

Debra paused to slip her long blond hair into a ponytail. "You mean besides the first six weeks of the year? Besides the fact that you are now officially a senior?"

"Aaahhhhh!"

The scream made Clarissa jump, her heart pounding. "What on earth—"

Justin Thompson ran by, trailing damp papers from his spiral notebook. His head was soaking wet. A good-looking blond guy with an eyebrow ring chased after him, laughing.

Debra sighed. "Did Ty dunk Justin's head in the toilet again?"

"Who's Ty?" Clarissa asked, leaning against a locker.

"A transfer student," Debra said. "He's pretty wild."

"And he is cute!" Clarissa declared.

Then she saw Jennifer Fear and Josie Maxwell striding down the hall. She waved to them. The two girls waved back and disappeared into a classroom.

"Oh, no," Debra moaned.

"What? What is it?" Clarissa followed Debra's gaze. Josh Maxwell, Mickey Myers, and Matty Winger were heading toward them.

"Oh."

Debra turned to face the lockers and pretended to search for something in her backpack.

Whoa. I knew things were tense since Debra and Josh broke up, but not *this* tense, Clarissa thought. "Let's go. Before he sees us," she suggested.

"Too late." Debra said.

"Hi, Clarissa." Josh grinned. "You're back, huh?"

"Cool," Mickey added.

"Yeah," Clarissa replied.

"Hey, Deb," Josh said, his dark eyes not meeting hers.

"Hello, Josh."

"You know . . ." Matty clapped one hand on Debra's shoulder and one on Josh's. "There's so much love in this hallway. It's just *oozing* out of you guys!"

"Watch it, Matty," Josh warned him.

"Get away from me, Matty!" Debra shouted, shoving his hand off her shoulder.

"That was so lame," Mickey said, pulling Matty away.

Matty giggled. "Just trying to keep it light!"

Josh shook his head. "Sorry about that. I just came over to say hi, Clarissa." He glanced at Debra. "See you around, I guess."

"I guess," Debra repeated. She watched Josh weave his way down the hall.

Debra's probably sorry she cheated on him, Clarissa thought. "You want him back, don't you?"

Debra blinked. "Uh, no way. I mean, all he wants to do is control me."

"But Clark Dickson over *Josh*?" Clarissa said. "I still don't get it. Josh is smart, funny, and cute. Clark is just weird!"

"At least Clark doesn't care what other people think," Debra replied. "Come on, I have to pick up something at my locker."

"*There* she is!" a girl's voice cried out.

Clarissa and Debra turned.

Mira Block smiled at them, arms folded in front of her. Her long blond hair was teased high. She wore a tight black T-shirt and denim miniskirt that showed off her long legs.

"Nice outfit," Debra said sarcastically.

Mira ignored her and hugged Clarissa.

Clarissa knew that Debra and Mira didn't get along. Debra was always saying that you couldn't trust someone who's been behind the bleachers with practically every guy in the school.

But Clarissa admired Mira's confidence.

The way she could get any boy she wanted. Clarissa never really knew what to say to guys.

"I'm so glad you're back." Mira gave Clarissa another hug.

"This place wasn't the same without you."

"Yeah, right," Clarissa replied, rolling her eyes.

"I'm serious!" Mira cried. "In fact, Will said the exact same thing the other day."

Clarissa smiled. She had met Will Reynolds not long after Justine's funeral. There she was, sitting by Silver Pond, thinking about her sister. Will came by and said just the right things to make her feel better.

That was right before she went into Dr. Sayles's clinic. Clarissa was a little disappointed that Will didn't visit her there. But they did spend hours on the phone.

"Will is really psyched to see you, Clar." Mira peeled a stick of gum and stuck it in her mouth. "He e-mailed me at home this morning."

"He e-mailed you?" Debra asked. "Why is he e-mailing *you*?"

Mira shrugged. "We're friends."

The bell rang and the halls began to clear out.

"I'll see you guys at lunch," Mira said. "Later!" She waved over her shoulder and headed down the hall, heels clicking.

Debra shut her locker with a slam. "Will is e-mailing *Mira*?"

"I know what you're thinking, Deb," Clarissa said. "But they've been friends for a long time. Way before I even *knew* Will. If she wanted to go after him, she would have done it a long time ago. Besides, Mira would never do that to me."

"Whatever you say," Debra replied. "I have to get to homeroom. I'll see you at lunch."

Clarissa headed to the principal's office. He had asked her to stop by before first period.

The hall, clogged with students two minutes earlier, was now deserted. Clarissa shifted her backpack on her shoulder and smiled.

It was good to be back. Finally she could concentrate on her senior year. No more Dr. Sayles. No more clinic. No more discussions about grief.

Clarissa heard a shuffling noise behind her.

She didn't have a chance to turn.

A pair of rough hands clamped around her throat from behind.

Clarissa clawed at them. Gasped for breath.

No air.

Just the hands, wrapped around her neck.

Squeezing . . . squeezing . . .

Chapter TWO

C larissa screamed and wrenched herself out of the attacker's grip. She spun around. "Will!"

Will Reynolds grinned at her.

Clarissa punched him in the shoulder but couldn't help smiling back. "You scared me half to death, you jerk!"

"I think you'll live," he replied playfully. Then he kissed her on the cheek.

Clarissa gazed at him, smiling. *He's so hot,* she thought. *His hazel eyes, his chocolate-colored skin, his long brown dreads . . . Wait a minute.*

Clarissa pulled away and stared at Will.

"Will!" she exclaimed, gaping. "Where's your *hair?*"

Will snickered. "At the barbershop." He

ran his hand over the remaining stubble on his scalp. "I know. Cool, huh?"

Clarissa ran her hand across his head. "It feels so weird."

Will shrugged. "We needed to change the band's look. Grunge is so dead," he replied. "And we have a show next week."

Oh, yeah, the band, Clarissa thought. Will played guitar for Violent Argument. They played at a lot of places in Shadyside and even got a few gigs in Center City.

"I think I like it." Clarissa smiled and rubbed his head again. "It makes you look older."

"Yeah? What about the goatee?" He fingered the stubble on his chin.

"That needs work." Clarissa laughed. "Lots of it."

"Thanks." Will grinned, and Clarissa felt herself warm up inside again.

"We should go, Will," Clarissa said. "We'll get busted."

"So?" He leaned in and tried to slip his hands around Clarissa's waist. She giggled and squirmed away.

"I have to go to the principal's office!" she pleaded. "I know you don't care about getting in trouble. But I don't need it my first day back."

"Oh, okay," Will grumbled. "I'll see you later?" he asked.

"Definitely." Clarissa forced herself to turn

away, then headed toward the main office.

Clarissa smiled to herself. She finally felt home again. Back at Shadyside High with her friends. With Will.

Senior year was going to be great.

"How was your first day at school?" her father asked that night at dinner.

"Awesome," Clarissa replied, twirling some spaghetti onto her fork. "I got to see everyone. And I'm not as far behind as I thought."

"That's good," her father said, wiping his mouth and putting his napkin down. "You know, we've only got two days before Aaron arrives."

"Aaron?" Clarissa asked. "We're still going through with the adoption . . . after everything that's happened?" She glanced at her mother, who was staring down at her plate. "Mom? We're going through with this?"

Her mother didn't respond.

"Honey, I thought you were okay with all this," her father said.

"But that was months ago!" Clarissa cried. "Before Justine . . . " Clarissa shook her head. "Forget it," she muttered.

"Come on, Clarissa," her father said. "We need you to be honest. You've met Aaron. Spent time with him. I thought the two of you got along okay."

"I don't have a problem with Aaron, Dad," Clarissa declared. "Really."

"But you do have a problem with *something*," he replied.

Clarissa took a deep breath and nodded.

"What is it?" he asked.

"I'm just not sure about this whole *adoption* thing," she said. "I know you planned it a long time ago. But . . . since Justine's death . . . I don't know."

Clarissa was quiet for a moment. She didn't know how to say what she was feeling. Just tell them, Clarissa thought.

"It feels like Aaron is almost a . . . a *replacement*," she blurted out. "A replacement for Justine."

"Do you really think your parents are that *cold*?" Clarissa's mother cried. "We loved Justine. Nobody could take her place. Nobody!"

Clarissa's heart jumped. "I'm sorry," she choked out. "I know that you want us to get on with our lives, turn the page, all that stuff. But it's hard. Justine hasn't even been gone a whole year. It all seems to be happening so fast."

"You don't know what it's been like," her mother went on.

"Every day I go into Justine's room. Try to put her things in boxes. But I can't bring myself to do it. I just can't." She cradled her face in her hands and began to cry.

Clarissa felt a lump grow in her throat. What's going on? I thought Mom was the strong one in the family.

Clarissa's father put an arm around her mother. "This is nuts. Aaron needs parents. And maybe we need him." He gazed at Clarissa. "You know, he needs a big sister, too."

He's not the only one, Clarissa thought. But deep down, she knew she was being a little selfish. Aaron did need a home. "You're right. I'm sorry, Mom. I just . . . "

"It's okay," her mother said, wiping her tears.

"Why don't I clean out Justine's room for you," Clarissa suggested. "It might be good for me to go through her things. And I'll be all moved in by the time Aaron arrives."

"Moved in?" her father asked. "We thought Aaron would take Justine's room."

"But you said *I* could have Justine's room," Clarissa replied. "It's bigger, and it has a huge closet. . . . And it was Justine's. I should have it."

Her father cleared his throat. "It's too soon," he said. "You've only been out of the clinic two days. It might be too much for you. You might—"

"Slip?" Clarissa asked.

Her mother offered a weak smile.

"You and Dr. Sayles keep telling me I need to get on with my life," Clarissa replied. "Maybe it's time I did."

"Do you really mean that?" her father asked. "This is what you want?"

Clarissa looked him straight in the eyes. "It's important to me." But she didn't know why. She didn't really care that Justine's room was bigger. But for some reason she felt she needed it.

Her father sighed. "Okay, sweetheart. We'll try it."

"Thank you!" Clarissa cried. She scrambled out of her seat and kissed them both on the cheek. "You know, you guys are okay, no matter what everyone says about you."

"Oh, you're a riot," her father said. "Just make sure that your stuff is out of your room by Wednesday."

"No problem." Clarissa bounded up the stairs. She marched to the end of the hall. Stopped when she reached Justine's door.

Clarissa shook her head. She had to go in. It was her room now. Get on with your life, Clarissa told herself.

Slowly she reached out for the doorknob and turned it. The door creaked open.

Clarissa breathed in stale air and flicked on the light.

Two boxes overflowing with winter clothes were stacked in the far corner. The walls were still covered with pictures of fashion models, clipped from magazines. The bed was made. Photos of friends were still taped to the mirror over the dresser. Even Justine's hair dryer was plugged in.

Everything was the same.

Clarissa sat on the bed and closed her eyes. She used to spend so much time in here when Justine was alive. She would crack jokes while Justine got dressed to go out. Sometimes Justine would play her guitar. She was always very private about her music. Never played it for anyone—except Clarissa.

Clarissa opened her eyes and glanced out the door of her new room. The setting sun glowed through the window at the far end of the hall, casting weird shadows and bathing everything in an eerie orange light.

She blinked. Was something moving by the stairs?

Clarissa focused her eyes. "Guess not," she said to herself. She dragged herself up off the bed and crossed the room to Justine's white desk.

She picked up an old photo of the two of them. They were standing in front of the house, holding hands. Clarissa was five and Justine, six. Mom snapped it right before they left for school that day.

Clarissa sighed and placed the picture

back on the desk, remembering her first day of kindergarten.

Then a flash of movement caught her eye. In the hallway.

A shiver ran up Clarissa's spine. "Mom? Is that you?" she called out.

Silence.

A glowing figure stepped out of the darkness. A girl.

Clarissa's heart pounded. Her throat tightened.

No. It couldn't be.

The girl's eyes glittered in the eerie light.

"Justine!" Clarissa whispered.

Chapter Three

"Justine," Clarissa gasped again. Is it a dream? Am I in some kind of shock?

Justine's form hovered at the end of the hall.

Her neck tilted sharply to one side. Broken. The brown skin of her neck bulged with lumps where the bones poked out.

She was wearing the same outfit as the night she died. Black jeans and a gray T-shirt.

Clarissa shuddered. Why am I seeing this? Am I losing my mind?

Justine gazed down the stairs, a sad expression on her face.

Clarissa suddenly felt dizzy. Images of the night her sister died flashed through her mind.

Finding Justine at the bottom of the stairs. Calling 911. Being so scared she could hardly speak.

She saw it again. Clarissa got home on a Friday night. Came through the front door. Heard Justine on the phone with her ex-boyfriend, Eddie Robbins.

"I don't want to hear it, Eddie!" she cried.

Then a scream. A horrified scream.

Clarissa rushed to the kitchen. And there was Justine. Lying on her stomach. Her head twisted around so far that she gazed at the ceiling.

Her eyes dead and blank—staring up at Clarissa.

Clarissa's stomach lurched at the memory.

"J-Justine," she stammered, slowly creeping to the doorway. Her eyes drawn to the vicious purple bruise on Justine's neck. The lumpy skin. The head held at such a strange, frightening tilt.

Justine didn't answer. The ghost floated soundlessly down the hall toward the bedroom. Her face was a mask of pain. Her glowing eyes stared past Clarissa. Into the bedroom.

"Justine! Is it really you?" Clarissa asked in a whisper. "Why have you come back?"

Justine floated by.

"Justine?" Clarissa gasped.

Justine didn't stop. She didn't try to speak to Clarissa. She traveled toward her desk against the wall.

Clarissa followed her into the bedroom.

Am I having another nervous breakdown? she wondered. Am I hallucinating the whole thing?

Clarissa glanced back into the hallway and closed the door. I can't go back to the clinic. She slid the small, dead bolt into place.

"Oh, Justine," Clarissa pleaded, timidly taking a step forward. "Are you angry that I took your room? Is that why you're here?"

Justine didn't respond.

"Please, Justine," Clarissa begged. "Answer me."

Justine paused when she reached her desk. She put a hand out. Her hand passed right through the top drawer.

Then her face changed. A frantic expression.

Clarissa's heart pounded in her chest. "What is it?"

Justine's ghostly hand pawed at the desk drawer, passing through it over and over.

"What are you looking for?" Clarissa demanded. She joined her at the desk.

Justine's eyes followed Clarissa's movement.

"Let me help you," Clarissa whispered. She yanked open the drawer. Old notebooks from school were piled inside. She held each one up for Justine to see. "This one? Or this one?" she kept asking.

Justine stared blankly at them.

"No? What else is in here?" Clarissa

21

shuffled through the piles of tissues, pens, and paper clips.

Justine didn't respond. Clarissa tossed the pens down in frustration.

"What *is* it, Justine?" she moaned. "I can't help you unless you tell me!"

But Justine wasn't looking at Clarissa. Her gaze was locked onto the top of the desk.

Clarissa followed Justine's gaze. "What?"

Justine lifted her hand, and pointed to one of the notebooks Clarissa had dumped there.

"This?" Clarissa asked, holding up the notebook.

Justine's glittering eyes were wide and excited. Her mouth moved frantically. But no words came out.

Someone pounded on the bedroom door.

Clarissa jumped. Her heart shot up into her throat.

"Open up!" a girl's voice called.

Clarissa looked at the door. Not now! she thought. Justine needs me. What do I do? She glanced back at her sister.

Gone.

Justine was gone.

Chapter Four

C larissa frantically scanned the bedroom. But Justine's ghost had vanished.

"Clarissa!" A fist banged on the door. "Hey, open up!"

"W-who is it?"

"It's Deb!"

"And Mira!"

Clarissa took a deep breath. "Just a minute." She moved on wobbly legs to the door. She fumbled with the dead bolt and opened it.

"Are you okay?" Debra asked as they marched in. "What are you doing in *here*?"

Clarissa sighed. "It's my room now." If Justine doesn't have a problem with that, she thought.

"Why was the door locked?" Mira asked playfully. She glanced at the closet next to the door. "Is Will in here somewhere?"

23

"No," Clarissa said, still shaken from her sister's visit.

"Are you sure?" Mira teased.

"You're disgusting, Mira," Debra muttered. "Why do you always have to go there?"

"Lighten up, Deb," Mira replied.

"No," Debra snapped. "Can't you see something's wrong?" She put a hand on Clarissa's shoulder. "What's going on?"

Clarissa stared into Debra's warm green eyes. Could she tell her? Could she tell her what just happened? That she saw her dead sister's ghost?

"Nothing," she replied.

But Clarissa couldn't fake it. She collapsed on the bed and covered her face. "I . . . I think I just saw my sister."

"Excuse me?" Debra asked.

Clarissa sat up and gazed at her friends. "Justine was here."

Mira sighed. "What are you talking about?"

Clarissa strode to the bedroom door, closed and bolted it once again. "First, promise that you guys won't tell anybody," she demanded.

Debra nodded. "We promise."

"Yeah," Mira agreed. "What happened?"

Clarissa drew a deep breath. Then she explained everything. Right up to when they banged on the door.

Her friends didn't say a word.

"Please don't think I'm crazy," Clarissa begged.

"We know you're not," Debra assured her. She sat down on the bed next to her. "But this is . . . this is so *weird*. Stuff like this just doesn't happen, you know?"

"Of course I know!" Clarissa sank onto the desk chair. "That's why I'm so freaked out!"

"You've had a rough couple of days," Debra said. I bet you're really stressed out. Maybe you only *thought* you saw something."

"I *saw* her," Clarissa insisted, shivering. "She was looking for something."

Mira grabbed Clarissa's hand. "She's really shaken up, Debra. Maybe she *did* see Justine." She gazed into Clarissa's eyes. "What do you think Justine wanted?"

"She kept pointing at this," Clarissa answered, grabbing the notebook off the desk. "I think it's important."

"But it's just an English book," Mira said.

"Let's see it," Debra said.

Clarissa flipped open the cover. Justine's handwriting was tiny and neat. Just like Clarissa's.

But there was a difference in their note-taking style. Justine drew cartoons in the margins—caricatures of friends and teachers, complete with word balloons and funny comments. She wrote a nickname for each person under his or her picture.

"Who's that?" Debra asked, pointing at a cartoon.

"That's Eddie," Clarissa replied. "She used to call him Hammerhead."

She flipped to another page and found a drawing of a girl with a goofy expression on her face. The girl held out a giant, shiny apple. The word balloon above the girl's head read, "It's so easy to please Mom and Dad. What's your problem?"

Beneath the drawing, she'd scrawled the name "Moon Girl."

"Moon Girl," Mira said. "Who's that supposed to be?"

"Justine used to call me that. It was her private name for me. Nobody else knew about it. Not even our parents."

"Why Moon Girl?" Debra asked.

Clarissa sighed. "She said I was so shy that I must be from the moon. It's stupid. I know."

Justine would never believe how much I've changed in two months, Clarissa thought. That I even have a boyfriend.

"What's that?" Debra asked, breaking Clarissa's thoughts.

Something sticking out of the back of the notebook. A slip of paper. Clarissa pulled it out and unfolded it.

RENATA
ASK HER ANYTHING

FOR SHE KNOWS THE FUTURE

Below that was a drawing of a fortune teller staring into a crystal ball. At the bottom was a 900-number. Clarissa turned the paper over and found a note in Justine's handwriting:

Call back August 20 @ 4:30 PM sharp!!!

A chill ran through her body. "That's the day after Justine died," she murmured.

"Weird," Mira said.

Debra flipped through the rest of the pages. "There's nothing else but English class notes in here."

"Then this has to be it," Clarissa said, reading the paper again.

"*What's* it?" Debra asked.

"The flyer. This must be what Justine wanted."

Clarissa paced the room. She studied the ad. It looked cheap. Silly. Still, Justine took Renata seriously enough to call her. And Justine's ghost had pointed at that notebook.

"Maybe Justine wants me to call Renata," Clarissa said. "Maybe Renata can tell me why my sister came back."

"Do you really think she could?" Mira asked.

Clarissa glanced at Debra.

"I still say you're stressed out," Debra said. "But it couldn't hurt to call, right?"

Rrriiinnnggg!

Clarissa jumped.

"That's me," Mira said. She opened her backpack and answered a cellular phone. "Hey!" She smiled and murmured something into the phone.

"Here we go again," Debra muttered.

"Uh-huh," Mira said, giggling. "That sounds like fun. I'll meet you at the Fear Street Cemetery in twenty minutes."

Clarissa and Debra exchanged glances.

"I have to go soon," Mira said, hanging up the phone. "So if we're going to call Renata, let's do it now."

"To ·the cemetery?" Debra asked. "Isn't that a little *weird*?"

"Don't get me started on weird." Mira crossed her arms. "At least the guys I go with don't have fangs or wear black capes."

"Give me a break with the vampire stuff," Debra sighed. "Clark is perfectly—"

"Hey, guys!" Clarissa interrupted. "We're calling Renata, remember?" Clarissa picked up Justine's cordless phone from the cradle on the nightstand. She hit the "on" button and heard a dial tone.

Mira and Debra crowded around her, waiting to listen in.

Clarissa punched in the number. Then she clicked on the speakerphone.

"It's ringing," Mira said.

Once. Twice. Three times.

Clarissa half expected a machine to pick up. But none did.

Then the ringing stopped. Faint static sounded from the speaker.

"Hello?" Clarissa asked. "Is anybody there? Renata?"

More static.

A chill crept up Clarissa's spine. I should hang up, she thought. But something is telling me not to.

"Hello?" a voice rasped over the speaker-phone.

Clarissa didn't know what to say. What did she expect this woman to tell her? "Um, I—"

"Moon Girl?" the voice asked.

Clarissa's eyes widened. She gaped at Debra and Mira. "Justine?" she asked.

"Can't talk long," Justine replied. "Too hard. Not enough . . . energy."

"What is it?" Clarissa cried. "Why did you come back?"

"Can't rest . . . "

Tears welled in Clarissa's eyes. She wanted to tell Justine how much she missed her. How she thought about her every day. "Ever since your accident I—"

"Nooo," Justine moaned, her voice a little weaker. "Pushed . . . two hands . . . behind me . . ." Her voice trailed away.

"But you fell down the stairs," Clarissa said. "I found you. It was an accident."

Mira grabbed Clarissa's hand.

"It *was* an accident, right, Justine?" Clarissa demanded in a trembling voice.

All she heard was a quiet hissing sound.

"Right, Justine?"

Then she heard something else. Very faint. Justine's distant whisper.

"Moon girl . . . I was *murdered*."

urdered!" Clarissa's mind whirled. Did someone push my sister down the stairs?

"Justine!" she cried.

No answer.

"I—I think she's gone," Mira whispered.

Debra put a hand on Clarissa's arm. "You okay?" she asked.

Clarissa shook her head and trembled. "This can't be happening."

Then a cough sounded over the speaker-phone. "Ohhhhhhh," a woman moaned. "Clarissa . . . are you still there?"

"Justine?" Clarissa asked.

"No," the voice replied, out of breath. "I am Renata."

"Renata?" Clarissa asked. "But, I thought—"

"What's going on?" Mira asked.

"Justine just spoke through me," Renata said.

"Right," Debra said. "What are you trying to pull?"

"Nothing. I—I . . . It's never happened this way before," Renata replied. "Usually I call to the spirits. But Justine took over my body. She must be very upset."

"You have to get her back for me, Renata!" Clarissa cried into the speakerphone. "I have to find out who killed my sister!"

"I can't," Renata replied. "I have no strength left."

"We'll come over there," Mira said. "Maybe that will make it easier for you."

"That's impossible," Renata replied. "I'm in New Mexico. You live in . . . Shadyside, right?"

"How did you know that?" Clarissa asked.

"Caller ID," Debra muttered. "Look, Renata, I think you're totally scamming us. Keeping us on the phone so you'll make some money. You probably have a whole database on Justine. And I think it's really sick of you to mess with Clarissa's head."

Maybe Debra is right, Clarissa thought. I miss Justine so much, I'll believe anything. Clarissa raised her hand to click the "off" button.

"Clarissa, don't hang up!" Renata shouted.

Startled, Clarissa pulled her hand back. "How—"

"You have to take Justine's return seriously," Renata said. "It takes great energy to contact the living. Even greater effort to *speak* to us. Justine must need your help."

"I don't know. . . ." Clarissa sighed.

"I'll prove to you that I'm the real thing," Renata said. "I will tell you about a secret you've kept to yourself. But you must take me off speakerphone."

Clarissa picked up the receiver. "Okay, Renata," she breathed. "I'm ready."

"I didn't want your friends to hear this," Renata said gently. "But you've had a crush on a boy named Josh for quite a while, haven't you?"

Clarissa's eyes opened wide. Debra and Mira stared at her.

"How did you know that?" Clarissa murmured into the phone. She turned away from her friends. "I mean, I never told anyone. Not even *Justine*."

"I don't know how these things come to me," Renata replied. "You just have to trust me. To put your sister to rest. Do you trust me, Clarissa?"

Clarissa nodded. "Yes."

"Good," Renata said. "Call me tomorrow night—around the same time. And have your friends there, too. The extra energy might be

33

the reason why Justine's connection was so strong."

"Don't worry," Clarissa replied. "I will."

The next afternoon, Clarissa stared at the clock in her calculus class. She tried to force the frightening call out of her head. Tried to think about something else. But she couldn't.

My sister was murdered, Clarissa thought.

She pictured Justine's ghost hovering by the stairs. Her twisted, purple neck. Her desperate face.

It's true, she thought. It has to be true. Why else would Justine come back?

The bell rang. Clarissa gathered her books.

She was supposed to meet Will at Pete's Pizza after school. Later, Mira and Debra had promised to come by Clarissa's house. She checked at the clock again on the way out of the classroom. Five more hours until we call Renata.

When Clarissa arrived at Pete's, she spotted Mira by the take-out counter. Standing next to Mira was that blond guy with the eyebrow ring. Ty.

Mira glanced at Clarissa, and motioned to the other side of the restaurant. Clarissa followed Mira's gaze and saw Will sitting in a booth by himself.

Should I tell Will about Justine? she wondered.

Would he still want to go with me if I told him I spoke to my dead sister?

Will caught sight of Clarissa. He flashed her a smile.

Clarissa melted. No way, she thought, heading toward the booth. No way am I going to tell him about it now. Maybe later.

"I don't think I'll ever get used to that hair," she said, trying to sound cheerful as she slid into her seat. "When I was in the clinic, I always imagined playing with your dreads."

"I could get a reggae wig for those . . . tender moments," Will said, laughing.

"Ha ha," Clarissa groaned. She leaned across the table to give him a kiss on the cheek.

Will tilted forward and brushed his lips against her mouth instead. Clarissa liked being close to him. Liked that they didn't have to talk on the phone all the time.

But it's almost *too* good. Were things moving too quickly?

She turned to see Josie Maxwell next to the table. Josie wore an apron over a Pete's Pizza T-shirt, and a red cap on her head.

"You guys want something to eat?" she asked.

"How about a pepperoni pizza and some Cokes, Josie?" Clarissa said.

Will put his lips on the end of a straw and blew the wrapper at her. Clarissa batted it away.

"No problem," Josie said and walked away.

Clarissa spotted Trisha Conrad across the restaurant. She sat by herself, reading a fashion magazine.

"Trisha!" she called out. They weren't great friends, but Clarissa wanted to ask her something.

Trisha glanced up. Clarissa waved her over.

"What's up?" Will asked. "You need a loan?"

"Hey, she's nice," Clarissa scolded him.

"It's easy to be nice when your dad owns the planet."

It was no secret that Trisha's father was the richest man in Shadyside. But Clarissa didn't care about that. She knew that Trisha sometimes had psychic visions.

"Hi, Clarissa. What's up?" Trisha flipped her long blond hair behind her shoulders.

"I was hoping I could talk to you," Clarissa said.

"What about?"

"Well . . . it's kind of weird. Debra Lake mentioned to me a while ago that you have, um . . . visions?"

Trisha's face darkened. "Why would she say that?"

"Yeah, why would she?" Will added.

36

Clarissa scowled at Will. "Look, Trisha, don't take it the wrong way. I'm not trying to make fun of you. I was just wondering, you know . . . what it was like."

Trisha slid into the booth next to Clarissa. She leaned forward. "You better not be joking around."

"No, I swear," Clarissa promised. "I'm just curious."

"Do you still think the senior class is doomed?" Will asked, chewing on the straw. "That we're all going to die?"

Trisha scowled. "I shouldn't have told anyone about that. The whole school thinks I'm crazy."

"I don't," Clarissa murmured. "Sometimes I wonder if it's true. I mean, we've had so many weird deaths already this year. They're even talking about putting up a memorial wall in the auditorium."

"Those were just coincidences," Will said. "We don't have some weird curse on us. Who really believes in that stuff anyway?"

Clarissa gazed across the table at Will.

And gasped.

Will's face contorted into a horrifying grimace. Two tiny veins on his forehead popped out as he stared into the distance.

His body shuddered violently.

"Will!" Clarissa cried. "What's the matter?"

Chapter Six

"**W**ill!" Clarissa repeated.

A piercing scream filled the restaurant.

Clarissa whirled around. She saw a woman sitting in a booth, her mouth wide in shock. She was drenched in soda!

Josie Maxwell stood next to her, frantically pulling napkins out of the dispenser. Josie had dumped a whole tray of drinks on the woman!

Will burst out laughing. "Oh, man, I couldn't hold it in anymore. That lady is so steamed!"

"That's twice today," Trisha said, with a giggle. "Josie dumped a whole Pete's Deluxe on Jade Feldman just before you guys got here."

"I bet Jade got free food for that one," Will said.

But Clarissa didn't want to talk about that. "Do you believe people can come back from the dead?" she blurted out.

Trisha's eyebrows shot up.

"Excuse me?" Will asked.

"I'm just curious," Clarissa replied. "Like with psychics. Do you think they can really channel the dead?"

"I don't know," Trisha replied with a shrug. "My flashes come out of nowhere. Sometimes they're right. Sometimes not."

Trisha's gaze moved to the door. Gary Fresno ambled in. He caught Trisha's eye and waved.

"Got to go," Trisha said. "I'm meeting Gary." She slid out of the booth and returned to her table. "Call me later—if you want!" she shouted to Clarissa.

Will's eyes widened. He stared over Clarissa's shoulder with a look of horror.

He covered his head with his coat and ducked for cover. "Look out!" he screamed. "It's Josie!"

"You're about as funny as a cold sore," Josie grumbled. She plopped their tray of pizza down on the edge of the table. "Give me ten bucks, or the next one's on you—literally!"

Will laughed and fished the money out of his pocket. Then they ate their pizza without mentioning Clarissa's sudden interest in Trisha's flashes.

"Walk you home?" Will asked after they'd finished.

"I guess you're allowed," Clarissa replied, slipping her arm through his.

The air felt chilly. The setting sun reminded Clarissa of the same orange glow that surrounded Justine's ghost when she first saw it.

"So what's with all the questions about psychics?" Will finally asked her.

Clarissa didn't know what to say. They were having such a good time. She *wanted* to tell Will about Justine. But she was afraid. Would he believe her?

Clarissa shook her head. It's now or never. "You have to promise me you won't think I'm weird," she said.

"I promise," Will replied.

"Or crazy. Or stupid. Or gullible . . ." she added.

"I promise," Will said. "Tell me."

"Okay," Clarissa said carefully. "Um . . . last night, Debra, Mira, and I called a psychic."

Will rolled his eyes. "Please don't tell me that you're into that stuff."

"No, I'm not *into* it," Clarissa replied. "There was a reason. . . ."

Will stared into her eyes. Waiting.

"Justine," she said.

Clarissa felt Will's body tense up, but she didn't want to let go of his arm. "What about her?" he asked.

Here goes nothing, she thought. "I . . . talked to her."

"You *talked* to Justine. Your sister."

Clarissa nodded. "The psychic channeled her."

Will sighed. "This is a joke, right?"

Clarissa's stomach tightened. "You said you'd listen. . . ."

"Come on, Clarissa," Will said.

"Please, Will, hear me out."

Clarissa told him about Justine's ghost. How it appeared out of nowhere. How it led her to Renata's number.

Will wouldn't even look at her. "So, what exactly did Justine say?" he asked.

"That she was pushed down the steps," Clarissa replied softly. "Murdered."

Will shook his head. "You actually *believe* this stuff?"

"I believe it," Clarissa replied. "But I can see that you don't. I'm sorry I said anything."

"What do you want me to say?" Will asked. "If I told you I believed you, I'd be lying."

Clarissa pulled her arm from his and fought back the tears. "I trusted you, Will. Trusted you to understand."

Will sighed. "You can't expect me to believe in ghosts and psychics. I mean, think about it. You spoke to your dead sister's *ghost*? Give me a break."

"It happened!" she cried shrilly.

"Okay, fine," Will said. "So let's say Justine was murdered. What are you going to do?"

"I don't know. I can't go to the police," Clarissa replied. "They'd never believe me."

"No kidding. They'd lock you up. Then they'd lock me up just for knowing you."

Clarissa wanted to scream. "Thanks for nothing." She tried to move past him.

Will put his hands on her shoulders. He gazed into her eyes. "I know how much you miss Justine. But you can't *really* believe all this. Promise me you won't call that psychic again."

Clarissa shrugged off his hands and backed away. "I can't promise," she replied sharply. "I'm calling Renata tonight. And I'm going to find out who killed my sister!"

"Hey," Mira said, dumping her backpack in a corner of Clarissa's room later that evening. She glanced at Clarissa. "You okay?"

Clarissa nodded. "Where's Deb?"

Mira shrugged. "I'm not her mother. I bet she's out with Count Clarkula. Maybe she won't even show."

"She'll be here," Clarissa replied.

"She makes me so angry sometimes." Mira scowled. "She's always in my face about going out with so many guys." Mira flopped down next to Clarissa. "But, I mean, she's the one who cheated on her boyfriend. What a hypocrite!"

"Maybe she says that stuff to make herself feel better," Clarissa offered. "I think she feels guilty about dumping Josh."

"She should," Mira said. "At least *my* guys *know* they're not the only ones."

Clarissa sighed. She hated conversations like this. She had them with both Mira and Debra. One was always talking about the other. Clarissa knew that Mira and Debra were friends with Clarissa, and *not* with each other.

"I kind of mentioned Renata to Will," Clarissa said, changing the subject.

"He didn't believe you, right?"

Clarissa shook her head. "We had a fight about it."

"Actually, I know," Mira said.

Clarissa raised her eyebrows. "You do?"

Mira didn't reply for a moment. Then she spoke carefully. "Will e-mailed me tonight. Before I came over here."

Clarissa narrowed her eyes. "Really? What did he say?"

"He's worried about you," Mira replied. "He asked me to talk you out of this."

Clarissa's insides felt twisted and tight. "What did you tell him?"

"That I was in on it, too. He thinks we're all

43

nuts. His exact words were, 1-900-HEAD-CASE."

Clarissa sighed. "Figures."

She climbed off the bed and glanced out the window. She had to admit that Will and Mira's relationship was starting to bug her. She wasn't happy that he went running to Mira as soon as they had a fight.

"Listen," Mira said. "Will and I have been friends for a long time. I hope you're not angry that we have this e-mail thing. I mean, there's nothing going on. Okay?"

Clarissa had to force a smile. "I know, Mira. Don't worry about it."

The doorbell rang downstairs. A few moments later Debra marched in. "My parents wanted to actually *see* that my homework was done before I went out," Debra grumbled. "Can you believe it? Like I'm a third grader."

"You guys ready?" Clarissa asked. "It's getting late."

"Let's do it," Mira replied.

Clarissa closed the door, bolted it, and scooped up the cordless phone. They huddled on the edge of the bed as she dialed.

Renata answered on the fifth ring.

"Renata . . . it's me, Clarissa."

"I know," Renata replied. "I'm glad you called. I'm sorry I couldn't help you yesterday. But you have no idea the strain that's involved."

"Is it always like that?" Clarissa asked.

"Especially with the first connection," Renata said. "But a spirit's power lessens with every contact. Sometimes I can't even channel them a second time."

"Are you saying that we might not even get to talk to my sister again?" Clarissa cried.

"Your sister's spirit is very powerful. I don't think we'll have a problem," Renata replied. "Let's begin. First you and your friends must hold hands."

Clarissa, Mira, and Debra did what Renata said.

"Now close your eyes and think of Justine. Get a strong picture in your mind."

Clarissa tried to think of a happy image, but she kept seeing her sister at the bottom of the stairs. Her neck snapped around. The blood dripping from her mouth.

She had to open her eyes.

Then Clarissa began to hear something. Low whispers. A rhythmic chant.

Renata's voice grew softer and softer. Soon it sounded like nothing more than heavy breathing.

"Renata?" Clarissa whispered. "What's happening?"

"Moon Girl?" a voice mumbled at last.

"Justine? Is that you?"

"Yessss . . . "

"Who did it, Justine?" Clarissa cried. She

45

didn't want to waste a minute. "Tell me. Who pushed you?"

"Don't know . . . Didn't see . . . "

Clarissa's heart sank.

" . . . pushed from behind . . . no time . . . "

"But why?" Clarissa pleaded. "Why would someone kill you?"

"No . . . something more . . . important . . . "

"What? How can you say that? What's more important?"

"You . . . "

"Huh?" Clarissa glanced at Mira and Debra.

"Must warn you . . . and your friends."

"Warn me?"

"My killer . . . won't stop . . . "

"What are you talking about?" Debra yelled into the phone.

"Tell us!" Mira cried.

Renata's voice gurgled and grew weak.

"Don't lose her, Renata!" Clarissa wailed. "Not now!"

"One of you," the voice continued, ". . . one of you . . . "

"What?" Clarissa urged her.

"Tell us, Justine," Mira repeated. "Tell us what you know!"

"One of you . . . will die."

Chapter Seven

"**S**he's gone," Renata gasped.

"Did you hear what Justine said?" Clarissa cried. "One of us is going to be killed!"

Debra and Mira sat rigid next to her, their eyes wide.

"Listen to me, Clarissa," Renata ordered. "Your sister has crossed a threshold. It's not easy for the dead to speak to the living. Justine reached out to warn you."

"But how could she know one of us will die?" Mira broke in. "She doesn't even know who killed her—"

"Spirits can see things we can't," Debra cut in. "Random events. Kind of like snapshots. The past, present, and future all mixed together."

"She's right," Renata replied weakly.

Clarissa gaped at Debra. "How do *you* know that?"

Debra smiled. "I did some reading over at Clark's last night."

"So what's it going to be?" Mira demanded. "An accident? Another murder? What?"

"I wish I knew," Renata told them. "Justine is the only one who can tell us that."

"Figures," Mira grumbled.

"What should we do, Renata?" Clarissa asked.

"Right now I need rest," the woman replied. "Maybe tomorrow we'll know more." She paused. "Until then, all three of you should be very, very careful."

Renata hung up.

Debra's face grew pale. "This is a nightmare. You don't think Justine's killer is really after us, do you?" She hopped off the bed and paced the room. "I mean, all of this . . . it's just so hard to believe!"

"I know this is crazy," Clarissa said. "But we have to take it seriously. We have to watch out for each other."

"It doesn't make any sense," Mira insisted. "Why would anyone want to kill *us*?"

"Why would anyone want to kill *Justine*?" Clarissa asked.

"I don't know," Debra replied. "But I'm scared." She dropped back down on Clarissa's bed.

"We have to do something," Clarissa declared. "We can't sit around and let someone stalk us."

"We have to find out who the killer is," Mira added.

"But how?" Clarissa asked.

"It can't hurt to ask around," Debra replied. "Maybe some of Justine's friends know something."

"They're all away at college," Clarissa pointed out.

Debra shook her head. "Not Justine's old boyfriend. I saw Eddie Robbins at the Corner last week. I'm going to talk to him."

"Well, I have to go," Mira said. "It's getting late. Come on, Deb. You can walk me home. Make sure no one murders us on the way."

"Great," Debra muttered, pulling on her jacket.

Clarissa showed them out.

What now? she asked herself as she returned to Justine's room. If only I could think of someone who didn't like Justine.

But Clarissa couldn't think of anybody. Justine had so many friends. Everyone loved her.

She glanced at Justine's desk. That's where the English book was. The book with Renata's flyer inside.

She picked up another notebook. Flipped

it open. Nothing. Just French notes. Then she searched through the rest of the desk. Looked in the dresser drawers and under the bed. No luck.

She made her way to the closet and pulled open the door. Clarissa glimpsed the boxes of Justine's clothes that she had shoved in the corner of the closet earlier that day. She climbed down onto her hands and knees, and pulled at one of the boxes.

It slid out a few inches, then caught on something.

She yanked harder. It wouldn't budge. The bottom had snagged on the edge of a wooden floorboard.

Great, the floor is rotting, she thought. She jiggled the box and pulled it out of the closet. Then she climbed into the closet to get a better look at the decaying wood.

But it was smooth. She pushed down on one end of the board with her hand. It moved.

It's loose, she realized. She shoved down harder.

The opposite end of the board popped up.

A secret hiding spot? Clarissa wondered. What was Justine hiding?

Clarissa slid her fingernails under the board. She lifted the wood with one hand and slipped her hand inside the crevasse with the other.

She felt some kind of plastic card. A credit card?

Clarissa pulled it out.

No. A driver's license. It had Justine's picture on it. But the name said Tania Adams. And Tania was twenty-one years old.

Cool, Clarissa thought. Justine had a fake ID. She placed the card on the floor and lifted the floorboard again.

This time her hand brushed against something cold and smooth. What's this?

Clarissa pulled it out—

And gasped.

Chapter Eight

Clarissa stared at a knife. A hunting knife in a black sheath. The word *SLASH* was printed on the leather.

She pulled off the covering. The sharp silver blade gleamed in the light.

Justine must have known she was in danger. Clarissa shivered. Why else would she be hiding this?

She stuck her hand back under the floorboard. There's something else in here. It feels like . . . a book?

The plain black cover crackled when she opened to the first page.

Justine's diary.

Clarissa's hands shook as she gripped the journal tightly. This might help me figure out who killed Justine!

She locked her bedroom door and sat down on the bed with the diary.

Clarissa took a deep breath. Forced herself to calm down. She picked up the remote to her CD player and clicked on some music.

Then she scanned the first page.

September 10: I hate school. I know it's my senior year, my LAST year, but I don't care. I won't make it to June at this rate. Physics, calculus, lit, they're all a joke. But it feels good, it feels okay to just let it all go. I don't care. I really don't. I flunked a test for the first time in my life last week. And it didn't hurt. I mean, it's supposed to HURT, right? Well, it didn't.

I didn't feel a thing.

The diary began at the beginning of Justine's senior year. Clarissa did the math. Justine started this diary less than a year before she died.

September 22: I did it. Finally. I waited until Mom and Dad were asleep and sneaked out the window. I, uh, BORROWED the car. I couldn't believe they didn't hear me backing out of the driveway. I thought I was nailed for sure. But their bedroom light never popped on. It felt so amazing. I picked up Slash and we drove around for hours. I mean, HOURS. We talked about everything. He's so beautiful. And he makes me feel so real. No one else ever has. I hardly even noticed that it was dawn when I got home.

I'm going to blow off school tomorrow. Sleep. How could I possibly take school after a night like tonight?

Who is Slash? Clarissa wondered. She stared at the hunting knife on the floor by her closet. She couldn't believe Justine was going with a guy who was into knives.

Stealing cars, ditching school. This wasn't the Justine she remembered. Maybe she didn't know her sister at all.

October 4: Hammerhead freaked when I told him off. I mean, I'm a senior now. It's not so weird to want to see other people, right? I can do whatever I want. Better believe it, Hammerhead. You don't own me. I couldn't believe he actually reminded me that he was captain of the football team and "could get any girl I want." Go ahead, hotshot. Get them all. You egotistical moron.

Weird. Justine had told Clarissa that Eddie Robbins dumped *her*. She seemed so upset about it.

October 19: Stole the car again. Mom and Dad must be deaf. Slash and I went to Zodiac in Central City. What a club! The fake IDs worked like a charm, and the band was kicking. My ears are still ringing. I could do this every night. Maybe I will!

P.S. Slash gave me a present tonight. A knife. It has his name on the leather cover. When he gave it to me, he called it "A token

*of my protection." He's so cool. A real poet. I
asked him why he gave me a knife as a gift.
He said, "Because flowers die."*

*November 8: Moon Girl told me Mom and
Dad freaked when they got up and realized I
didn't come home last night. Oh well. Moon
Girl lied, of course (I trained her well). She
said that she forgot to tell them I slept at
Glamour Girl's house. Way to go, Moon Girl.
She asked me later where I really was last
night, but I told her to mind her own business.*

*She's not mature enough to hear about all
this yet.*

*December 3: Slash hassled me about
Hammerhead. Well, so what if I'm still seeing
Hammerhead? He's my boyfriend, right? Slash
gave me the whole hurt-puppy speech: How
could you cheat on me, blah, blah, blah. I told
him we're still just friends, no matter what he
thinks. Slash started yelling—he scared me.
He said I'm ashamed of him. That's why I kept
our friendship a secret. Am I? No. But I told
him we needed to be free to sneak out at night
and hit the clubs. Music is the only thing that
matters now. He agreed. That shut him up—
for now.*

*Slash had been so mellow until now. I didn't
see this coming. Maybe I should've—he gave
me a KNIFE after all. I'll have to watch him.
Didn't think he was the jealous moron type.*

December 9: I can't believe it! Slash rented

time for me in a recording studio in Center City! He wants to make up for being a jerk the other night. Consider yourself made up, Slash! What a gift! Better than a knife! I'm dying to cut a demo! Pretty soon I'LL be the one up on stage.

December 16: Auditioned for the band today. Some other guitarists I knew were there. Some good players. I was totally freaked. But I managed to play two new songs. They told me I was good, but I don't know. They could've just been saying that. They also said my stuff didn't have enough of an edge. Well, maybe it doesn't. . . . I don't care. I wasn't going to let them see how much that hurt.

In case you can't tell, I'm crying right now. . . .

I thought I knew Justine as well as she knew herself. But she had totally shut me out of her life. If only she would have let me in, Clarissa thought. Let me see who she really was. Maybe I could have helped her. Maybe she'd still be alive.

December 21: Hooked up with Slash after school. School. What a joke. We walked down to Fear Lake and skipped a few stones, trying to break through the ice. Then we sat on one of the benches. That's when Slash gave me my Christmas present. That necklace. It must have cost him a fortune.

It was so beautiful. But I couldn't accept it. It

just wasn't right. It was too much. He insisted I take it, but I said no way. I told him to give it to some other girl who was good to him. Not like me. He freaked out, telling me there wasn't anyone else who was good to him. There was no one but me. The necklace was MEANT for me, and if I didn't want it, he would throw it away. Then he tossed it in the lake! I told him he was crazy.

Sometimes I wonder . . . IS HE?

January 22: Slash found out I went out with Strummer, that bass player from Zodiac. He went nuts again. Why did I go out with every guy but HIM? Everything was cool until he shoved me. Hard. I almost fell over. No one's ever touched me like that! I kicked him as hard as I could. Got him good. Then I took off. He went too far this time, and I'm not going to take it. Let him rot. I don't need HIM.

He shoved her? Clarissa gaped at the words of the diary. This Slash guy was pushing Justine around? She always seemed so together—so happy.

February 4: Dad tried to nail me for that parking ticket I got in Central City last month. He played it off so innocently, "I can't figure out why I got this ticket in the mail. I mean, it was written in the middle of the night. In Central City, no less. I just don't get it." HA! He watched me the whole time for my reaction. But duhhhh. I don't have a clue, Dad, I told him. Maybe you were sleep-driving.

February 12: Slash won't leave me alone. He calls me at three in the morning to make sure I'm home. Mom and Dad would be all over me if they found out. I turned off the ringer on my phone.

Now Slash is starting to hang out across the street, watching me through my window.

Clarissa put the diary down and crept closer to the window. She had a clear view of the front yard and of the house across Fear Street. "Slash is a total psycho!"

He used to watch Justine from across the street, she thought. Right from behind that big maple tree. She glanced back at the knife lying on the floor by the closet.

Maybe he killed her, Clarissa thought.

A chill ran down Clarissa's spine.

Her sister's killer wasn't finished.

One of you will die. . . . That's what Justine had said. Was Slash the one who was following her? Was he out there? Waiting?

Clarissa stared at the tree for another minute.

No. No movement.

"You're just freaking yourself out, Clar," she said under her breath. "Imagining things."

Clarissa sat back on the edge of the bed and kept reading.

February 14: I got a package today. Told my parents it was some clothes I ordered from a catalogue. But I lied. It was a dead bird. Happy Valentine's Day to you, too, Slash.

Slash is a complete maniac! I wish Justine wasn't so hung up on nicknames. I have to find out who he really is, Clarissa thought. Maybe Renata can help.

March 8: The audition cooked. I could really get this gig. And if I do, that's it. I'm going to do it. Drop out of school. Leave it all behind. No more family, no more Slash, no nothing. That's what I need.

Maybe I'll even be happy.

Clarissa's mouth went dry.

Justine wanted to run away? The only time she ever talked about leaving home was when she filled out those college applications. She even said that the only thing she'd regret about going away to school was how much she'd miss Shadyside. And her little sister.

That meant so much to me, Clarissa thought, tears stinging her eyes. But Justine was lying.

March 16: I've had it with men. Slash. Hammerhead. They think they can treat me like—

Clarissa heard a *thud*. Outside her window.

She lowered the volume on the CD player and listened.

The roar of a car driving down Fear Street. That's it.

Don't be so paranoid, she told herself.

But Justine's warning came flashing through her mind again.

One of you will die.

What if she was the one?

Clarissa heard a soft scraping sound.

No mistake. It came from outside the window.

She ran to the light switch and clicked it off.

There it was again. Louder this time.

She crouched down on the floor. The glow from a streetlight cast shadows across her bed and carpet.

It's nothing, she reassured herself. Probably just a tree hitting the side of the house . . . right?

In the darkness, Clarissa gazed through the window. Watching. Listening to the scraping sounds. Growing louder . . . louder. Then she gasped in horror.

A dark shape. Faceless. Silhouetted by the streetlight.

She tried to scream, but no sound came out.

Clarissa could only sit. Frozen.

Staring at the window. Staring at the two gloved hands slowly sliding it open.

Chapter Nine

Clarissa couldn't move. Her heart pounded. Her mouth went dry.

She needed a weapon.

The knife!

She snatched it from the floor by her closet. She popped the snap and slid it out of the sheath. The metal glinted in the dim light.

The window rose silently.

The figure slipped through. First one foot, then the other.

"Stay away from me!" Clarissa cried hoarsely. "I mean it! I have a knife!"

"It's me, Clarissa. Why did you turn the lights off?"

"Will?" She fumbled for the light switch and clicked it on.

"What on earth are you doing?" she

whispered harshly, not wanting her parents to hear. "Are you crazy? You scared me to death!"

He shrugged. "Sorry. I didn't mean to. I saw you through the window and—" His gaze fell on the knife. His eyes narrowed. "Where did you get *that*?"

"It's Justine's," she told him. "I found it."

Clarissa's fear turned to anger. The last thing she needed was to continue her fight with Will. "What do you want, Will?"

He sighed. "I acted like a jerk today," he said, staring down at his feet. "I wanted to apologize."

Clarissa let out a breath of air. "So what's wrong with the front door?"

"I thought it would be more fun this way." He glanced at the knife in Clarissa's hand and smirked. "Are you going to stab me or what?"

"I should," she muttered as she slipped it back into the sheath and placed it on the desk. "I thought someone was breaking in."

"What? To *kill* you?" he asked with a note of sarcasm. Then he took off his gloves and shoved them into his jacket.

Clarissa glared at him.

"I talked to Mira," he said, sitting down on the edge of the bed. "She e-mailed me after she got home from your last call to the psychic hotline."

62

A wave of anger passed through Clarissa. "Mira e-mailed you? She was the one who didn't want to tell anybody! Why doesn't she just pick up the phone, anyway?"

Will shrugged. "She thought it was okay to tell me. Since I knew about it anyway. . . . So, this Renata lady really has you guys going. I'm worried about you."

"So you said," Clarissa replied coldly. "Because you care about me, right?"

"You make it sound evil." Will moved closer to Clarissa. "Don't be that way," he said softly, wrapping his arms around her waist.

Clarissa rested her head on Will's shoulder. She wanted to stay angry at him. But her body began to relax. She closed her eyes. "Do you know what my parents would do if they knew you were here?"

"Kill me?" he asked.

"Yes," Clarissa said. "*And* me. You can't stay here. They'll hear you."

"No, they won't," he whispered. "And I don't want to leave yet. Tell me about tonight. Where did the knife come from?"

He picked it up and ran his fingers over the name Slash.

"Oh, *now* you want to know." Clarissa narrowed her eyes. "Why?"

"I just want to know how you're doing," Will replied.

Clarissa picked up Justine's diary and

tossed it to him. "*That's* how I'm doing."

Will caught the book and looked at Clarissa.

"Justine's diary," she said.

"A diary?" He opened it and skimmed the first few pages. "What's it say?"

"A *lot*." Clarissa sighed. "Stuff that makes me feel as if I never knew Justine at all."

"You told me you guys were close."

"That's what *I* thought," Clarissa said. "But she had a whole other life. She'd sneak out in the middle of the night and hit the clubs in Central City. She'd steal our parents' car and blow off school. She wanted to drop out."

"I've played at some of those clubs," Will commented. "They can be pretty rough."

"The only thing she cared about was her music—any music," Clarissa said. "All because of this guy Slash."

"*Slash*?" Will replied, still thumbing through the diary. "Sounds like a real winner."

"That was her nickname for the guy. I don't know his real name. But from what Justine wrote about him, he's a total psycho."

Will snickered. "I know a lot of those club clowns. Most of them are all talk. But let me guess. You think he had something to do with her death, right?"

"I think so," Clarissa said. "I have to find out who he is. I'm going to ask Renata to help me."

"Oh, right," Will muttered. "You'll get all your answers from a psychic hotline."

Clarissa balled up her hands. "Renata is *different*," she said. Her cheeks grew hot.

"Sure she is," Will said.

"Don't you even *care*?" Clarissa cried. "Maybe you will when one of us dies." She leaped to her feet. "What if it's Mira? Then who will you send e-mails to?"

Will stared at her. "Are you steamed because of *that*?" he asked. "Come on, Clarissa. Mira and I take computer class together. But that's as far as it goes."

Clarissa sighed. "I know. I believe you. It's just that she—"

"Gets around?" Will asked.

"That's *not* what I meant," Clarissa said.

"Then what *did* you mean?" he demanded, getting up.

Clarissa fidgeted. "It's just that . . . she's . . . so beautiful. And funny. And sexy."

Will stepped forward. "So are you," he said in a soft voice.

Clarissa couldn't meet his eyes. "No, I'm not."

His arms slipped around her waist again. He pulled her close. "You're trembling," he whispered.

"I . . . I'm scared," Clarissa said. "I'm telling you, Will. This whole thing with my sister . . . it's *real*."

Will nodded. "I believe that *you* believe it. I just hope you're wrong."

"Me, too," Clarissa replied softly and hugged him close. Will pressed his lips against hers, and Clarissa kissed him back. It feels so good in his arms, she thought. I just wish he believed me.

"Look. I'll ask around at my next gig," Will said softly. "See if we can find—"

Someone pounded on the bedroom door.

Clarissa jumped.

Will's eyes opened wide.

"Clarissa? You in there?"

"Dad!" Clarissa gasped. She put a finger to her lips, warning Will to be quiet. Then she grabbed his arm and shoved him toward the closet.

The bedroom door rattled.

"Clarissa?"

"Yeah, Dad," Clarissa called out. She shoved Will into the closet. He slid the door closed.

"Why is this door locked?" her father demanded.

"Hold on," Clarissa said, rolling across the bed and unbolting the door in one motion.

Her father entered. "You okay in here? I thought I heard voices."

"Voices?" Clarissa asked innocently. "Maybe you heard this." She picked up the stereo remote and turned up the CD.

"No, that's not it," Dad remarked. "I thought I heard a *boy's* voice."

"I think you're hearing things, Dad," she replied.

He raised an eyebrow. "Maybe I am." He ran his hand over the dead bolt on the door. "I never liked this lock. I can't believe Justine talked me into installing it."

"*I* like it," Clarissa replied.

"So I see." Her father paused. His eyes narrowed. "Why is the window open? It's October. It's freezing in here!"

Clarissa rolled her eyes and groaned. "I just wanted some fresh air."

"Okay, okay," her father replied. "Just close it before you go to bed, please."

"No problem." Clarissa smiled sweetly.

"I also want to let you know about tomorrow."

"What's the deal?" Clarissa asked.

"We're bringing Aaron home around dinnertime," her father said. "It's going to be a long day of signing papers and red tape. I'd appreciate it if you'd have some food here for us. Pizza, Chinese take-out, or something. I'll leave you money on the kitchen table. . . . Oh—and no friends over tomorrow night."

"But, Dad, we had plans!" *Plans to contact my dead sister,* she thought.

"Break them. It's a family-only night," he said. "Seems as if those two girls have been *living* here lately."

Clarissa nodded. "Fine."

"Great. Good night, honey." He kissed her forehead and shut the door.

Clarissa waited until his footsteps faded, then slowly slid the dead bolt back into place. Then she opened the closet door.

Will grinned at her from between two dresses.

"*Out*," she whispered and pointed to the window.

"I'm going," he replied, smiling sheepishly. "You know, you're cute when you're freaking out."

"*Out*," Clarissa repeated.

He slipped his gloves on and threw one foot over the windowsill. "Seriously, Clarissa. Lock this window after I leave. Any creep can climb up here."

Clarissa smiled. "Yeah, I know."

"I'll call you." He leaned back inside and gave her a quick kiss on the cheek.

Clarissa closed the window and watched him jog across the lawn out of sight.

Then she remembered Justine's journal.

There was more to read.

May 20: I can't take it anymore. I've been getting prank calls every night for weeks. Someone is watching me. Waiting for me. And now I'm starting to get really scared because—

Clarissa's heart thundered.

Someone was stalking Justine. Who? Slash?

She quickly turned the page.

But there was nothing there. No words.

The rest of the diary was blank.

I've got to do something, Clarissa told herself. I can't live with this mystery. And I can't live in fear for the rest of my life.

I can't tell Mom and Dad. They won't believe me about Renata, about Justine coming back. They'll think I've flipped out again.

But I've got to do something. How can I find out the truth?

Suddenly she had an idea.

Chapter Ten

Clarissa pulled the car into the crowded lot and found a parking space at the back. The red and blue neon sign blinked on and off, the light reflecting in her windshield.

ZODIAC . . . ZODIAC . . . ZODIAC.

She gazed at the blinking word, surrounded by red neon stars. "Are we really doing this?" she asked quietly.

Debra reached for the handle on the passenger door. "What's the big deal?" she asked. "We look twenty-one, don't we?"

"But we don't look anything like the photos on our fake IDs," Mira chimed in from the backseat. "If the guy at the door checks them carefully . . ."

"It's probably really dark in the club,"

Debra said. "Besides, lots of kids from school have been to this place with no ID at all. At least, they say they have."

Debra pushed open her door. The sound of dance music, pounding drums, a steady, repeated rhythm, floated out over the parking lot.

Clarissa swallowed hard. "Thanks for coming with me," she told them. "I know you think this is a crazy idea."

"Yes, we do," Mira replied without hesitating. "But it's an adventure—right?"

"And if this guy Slash is still hanging out here . . ." Clarissa started. "If I can see him . . . talk to him . . . "

"Then what?" Mira demanded.

Clarissa shrugged. "Then maybe I'll feel better," she murmured.

"We're not going to feel better about anything if we stay here in the parking lot," Debra said, pulling her coat tighter against the cold. "Come on. We're twenty-one, right? I'll treat you guys to a beer."

Mira rolled her eyes. "Big whoop."

Clarissa took a deep breath and climbed out of the car. In the next car she saw a couple kissing, completely wrapped up in each other. Turning to the door of the club, she saw two young men arguing loudly, waving beer bottles in their hands, shouting and gesturing.

The shrill wail of a siren rose and fell somewhere in the far distance. The door opened, and the pounding music from inside drowned out the sound of the siren.

Their shoes crunched over the gravel lot. Clarissa shivered. Her hand clenched around the fake ID card in her pocket, her sister's card, the one hidden under the floor.

Justine—can you see me now? she wondered. I'm doing this for you.

A skinny young guy with long, greasy hair and an unlit cigar in his mouth stopped them at the door. "IDs," he muttered, watching the two men arguing behind them.

The girls raised their cards. He waved them in without even glancing down at them.

Clarissa led her friends through the smoky, crowded room to a tiny round table near the back. On a small stage a band was setting up its amps. Recorded dance music blared from a speaker right behind their table.

Red and blue lights throbbed over a tiny dance floor. Just about every table was filled, and people stood three-deep at the bar.

Clarissa waited for her eyes to adjust. Then she gazed from table to table, searching for anyone she knew, anyone from Shadyside High.

No. Most everyone appeared older.

A waitress in a short black skirt and black tights took their drink order. They had to shout at the top of their lungs to be heard. The noise in the club was so loud it made Clarissa's ears ring.

Clarissa turned her attention to the band. A tall, lanky black guy was plugging cords into a keyboard, frowning and shaking his head unhappily. Two other guys wearing torn sweatshirts and jeans and wool ski caps on their heads were dragging a heavy amp across the small stage.

Clarissa heard a cry and the sound of shattered glass. Someone had dropped a drink on the floor. A few people clapped and cheered.

A young woman danced by herself on the dance floor, her eyes shut, body swaying, a drink in one hand.

This is a waste of time, Clarissa thought. What a stupid idea.

What made me ever think I could just drop in here and find Slash?

And what would I say to him if I *did* find him?

She jumped up, nearly toppling her chair over. "Be right back," she shouted to her friends. Mira and Debra were watching the band members set up.

Clarissa stopped a waitress. "Where is

the bathroom?" The waitress pointed.

Clarissa made her way past the swaying solitary woman on the dance floor. Then she followed a path through the jammed-together tables, past laughing couples and groups of young men moving their shoulders, bobbing their heads to the music.

"Hey—Hot Stuff!" someone called.

Hot Stuff? Was he calling to her? Clarissa didn't turn around.

A hand-printed sign—RESTROMS—with one "O" missing led her into a narrow dark corridor. The gray tiles on the wall and the low ceiling made it seem more like a tunnel than a hallway.

The sharp sting of ammonia greeted her as she turned a corner. She saw a half-open closet filled with cleaning supplies.

The music boomed far behind her now. The tunnel grew darker. Several bulbs were out. Her footsteps echoed hollowly on the concrete floor.

Clarissa gasped as a figure stepped into her path.

She stopped short and stared at a tough-looking young man, dressed all in black, his head shaved, his mouth curled in a sneer. He stared back at her without blinking, studying her coolly.

Her eyes locked on his. His eyebrows were pierced, she saw.

And in each eyebrow . . .

In each eyebrow . . .

No!

A tiny silver dagger.

Clarissa tried to slide past him. But he didn't move out of her way.

"How's it going?" he asked. Somehow he made it sound like a threat.

"Okay," Clarissa choked out. Again, she pressed her back against the wall and tried to slide past him.

A cold half-smile revealed a gold tooth in the front of his mouth. The dim light made the twin daggers gleam for just a moment as he tilted his head, studying her up and down.

"Fine . . . fine . . ." he murmured.

Clarissa swallowed hard and didn't reply. She couldn't take her eyes off the daggers in his eyebrows. Was it him? Was it Slash?

Did he get the nickname because of the daggers?

Am I staring at my sister's murderer?

"You're new?" he asked. His voice seemed to come from far away, as if out of a thick fog.

"No. Please," Clarissa choked out. "I— well . . . Let me pass. Okay?"

He chuckled, as if she had said something funny.

He didn't move out of the way.

Instead, he took a step toward her. Staring. Staring so hard.

"Come here. I've got what you want," he whispered.

Chapter Eleven

No!" Clarissa cried.

Her knees suddenly felt weak. Her hand shot out to the wall, as if trying to hold her up, keep her from falling.

The young man chuckled again. His dark brown eyes burned into hers, angry eyes, menacing eyes.

Dagger eyes, she thought.

"Let me go!" Clarissa pleaded.

And then someone else was behind her. She saw darting shadows. Heard an angry shout.

"Hey—what's the deal?"

Clarissa spun around—and saw Will.

Will, in a silvery sports shirt, hanging out over baggy black jeans. Will, his face tight with anger. Fists clenched at his sides.

The menacing young man backed up a step. Squinting at Will, he raised both hands as if in surrender. "Hey, no problem, Bro," he uttered.

"What's the deal?" Will repeated breathlessly, challenging the other guy.

"Everything's cool, Bro." He took another step back. "I thought she came down to . . . transact some business, that's all." He raised his hands higher. "But it's cool. It's all cool."

Will had Clarissa by the shoulders. He spun her around and guided her out of the tunnel. They stopped at the entryway to the main room.

"What are you doing here?" They both asked the question in unison.

Clarissa laughed. She held on to the front of Will's shiny sport shirt. "I was never so glad to see you. Will to the rescue! Where did you come from?"

"I'm here with my band," he told her. He nodded to some boys huddled together at the bar. "Those are my guys. I told you, we're playing here next week. We're just checking out the place."

"I'm so glad," Clarissa sighed. "I thought—"

"Let me guess why *you're* here," Will said, frowning. "You're looking for that Slash guy—right? You thought he'd sit down at your table and introduce himself."

Clarissa suddenly felt embarrassed.

"Maybe it wasn't so smart," she mumbled. She forced a smile. "At least I gave you a chance to be a hero."

Will didn't smile back. "Better get Mira and Debra and go home," he said, squeezing her icy hands. "It's rough here. Really."

He brought his face close to hers, so close she could smell the peppermint on his breath. "Don't come here, Clarissa," he whispered. "It could be dangerous."

Clarissa stared at him, feeling a chill.

Was he trying to keep her safe?

Or was that a threat?

The next evening Clarissa ordered a pizza around five o'clock. Soon after, she heard a car turn into the driveway. Her parents were home.

With Aaron.

Clarissa hurried to the bathroom to splash some water on her face. She gazed at herself in the mirror. "Ugh! Nice circles under your eyes, Clar," she whispered. "You'll probably scare the little guy away."

She brushed her hair, took a deep breath, and marched downstairs to say hello to her new brother.

Clarissa's father smiled when she entered the living room. He put a hand on Aaron's shoulder. "You remember Clarissa, don't you?"

"H-hello," Aaron stammered. He stared up at her with big brown eyes.

Clarissa wasn't sure how big five-year-olds were supposed to be. But Aaron looked small for his age.

"Hey, Aaron," Clarissa said, bending down to greet him. "What's up?"

Aaron didn't reply. He stepped back behind her father.

Clarissa saw the way his eyes darted nervously around the room. Noticed how tightly he clung to the stuffed bear in his arms. He was so scared.

Clarissa's heart melted. She knelt beside Aaron and pulled him close. "We're your family now. Don't be afraid."

Aaron hadn't been adopted until now because of his emotional problems. The reports said he fought with other kids. Threw horrible tantrums. Clarissa knew why. Her father told her. It was too terrible to think of.

Aaron had witnessed his own parents' murder.

They ran a diner a few miles outside of Central City, right off of the Cononka River. Aaron's father cooked and his wife waited tables. One night two guys walked in at closing time. They emptied the cash register.

But that wasn't all. The armed robbers pulled Aaron and his family out of the restaurant. They tied his parents up and pushed them into the river.

Aaron witnessed the whole thing.

Ever since then, Aaron had been deathly afraid of the water. He couldn't swim. Wouldn't even go near it. He had nightmares. And tantrums. And was generally disturbed.

"Can I watch TV?" Aaron asked.

"Sure thing," Mr. Turner said. "But let's have some dinner. Then you can watch all the cartoons you want."

Aaron smiled for the first time.

"Where's Mom?" Clarissa asked.

"She had to pick up something at the mall," her father replied. "Why don't you show Aaron his room?"

"Okay," she said. "You want to go upstairs, Aaron?"

He shrugged.

They climbed the stairs. Clarissa opened the door to her old room. "This used to be my bedroom," she explained, going inside. "But you'll sleep here now."

"This is mine?" Aaron skipped around the perimeter of the room, running his hands along the pale green wallpaper. His other hand remained tightly wrapped around the stuffed animal.

"Where do you sleep?" he asked.

"Come on," Clarissa replied. "I'll show you."

She led him to her new room down the hall. "This used to be Justine's room, but now it's mine," Clarissa told him as she opened the door.

"But where does Justine sleep?" he asked.

"Well . . . Justine's . . . gone away."

Clarissa crossed the threshold into her room, but Aaron's feet remained planted in the hallway.

"Don't you want to see?" she asked.

Aaron shook his head no.

"Who's that?" she wondered, pointing to the stuffed bear.

"Oscar," he whispered. "He's my friend."

"Why don't you and Oscar come on in?" Clarissa asked.

Aaron straddled the doorway for a moment, as if he was making sure nothing bad would happen.

Finally he stepped in.

"Justine is with my parents," he announced immediately.

Clarissa stared at the boy in shock. "How do you know that?" she asked.

Aaron shrugged. "My parents are in heaven. That's where dead people go." Aaron gazed around the room. "Hey, you have a phone and a computer and a stereo *and* a TV. Cool!"

He picked up the remote and flicked on the TV. Then he headed for the phone. Put the receiver to his ear. His nose wrinkled. "Huh?"

Aaron's body jerked. Oscar slipped from under his arm and hit the floor. Aaron let out a soft moan.

"Aaron?" Clarissa asked.

Aaron's eyes rolled up into his head. "Uhhhhh." He dropped the phone.

"Aaron!" Clarissa grabbed the boy's shoulders and shook him. Something's wrong with him, she thought. Really wrong. "Dad!" she screamed. "Dad! Come quick!"

Aaron's lips curled up, exposing his teeth. It looked as if he was trying to say something. But instead he made sharp, rasping sounds.

And then the boy spoke.

"Be careful . . . Moon . . . Girl."

Chapter Twelve

"Justine?" Clarissa cried. "Is that you?"

"Too late . . . another murder . . . too late . . ."

Justine is warning me, Clarissa thought. Another murder was about to happen. Or maybe it already had.

"Who?" Clarissa cried. "Tell me who's going to die!"

Aaron's whole body quivered. He let out a tiny moan and collapsed on the rug.

"Aaron!"

Clarissa leaned over him and put her ear to his nose and mouth. His chest rose and fell. His breath hit her cheek. Relief flooded her. He was breathing!

In fact, he looked peaceful. Almost as if he were napping.

"Dad!" Clarissa yelled. "Dad!"

Clarissa heard her father take the stairs two at a time. An instant later he knelt next to her and Aaron.

"What happened?" he asked.

"I—I don't know," she said. She couldn't tell him the truth. That she thought Aaron had just channeled Justine. Dad would send her back to the clinic for sure.

"Aaron," her father said, lightly slapping Aaron's cheeks. "Come on, Aaron. Wake up!"

Seconds passed. Aaron's eyelids twitched.

"That's it, Aaron," Mr. Turner whispered.

Aaron's lids fluttered, then opened. "What happened?" he asked.

"You're fine," Mr. Turner assured him, his voice filled with relief. "Just relax."

"Aaron is a little hypoglycemic," he explained to Clarissa.

"What's that?" Clarissa asked.

"Low blood sugar. It's not serious. Once we get some food in him, he'll be okay. Let's take him downstairs. Give him an orange before the pizza comes." He gazed at Aaron. "Okay?"

Aaron nodded.

Clarissa helped Aaron down to the kitchen. Then she raced to her father's study. And dialed Debra's number.

Three rings. Four.

"Come on, Debra, pick up."

Clarissa's heartbeat quickened with every ring. She tried to tell herself that it was dinnertime—Debra might not be allowed to answer the phone. But her mind imagined other things.

Horrible things.

Another murder, Justine had said.

What if the killer already—

"Hello?" came Debra's voice.

Clarissa breathed a sigh of relief. "It's me," Clarissa said. "Are you okay?"

"Of *course*," Debra replied. "What's going on?"

Clarissa explained what happened when Aaron picked up Justine's phone.

"Whoa," Debra murmured. "What does it mean?"

"What do you think? Justine is warning us, Debra! One of us is about to get killed!"

"Did you call Mira yet?"

"No. Dad just took Aaron downstairs. I haven't had a chance."

"This is so creepy, Clarissa." Debra's voice was full of dread. "I can't believe what's happening to us. It's almost as if . . . as if Trisha was right. Maybe the seniors *are* doomed."

"And we're next." Clarissa took a deep breath. "I should call Mira," she declared. "She needs to know what happened."

"Right. But before you do, I have to tell

you something. Guess who I saw at the mall after school today."

"Who?"

"Eddie Robbins!" Debra replied.

"Really?" Clarissa gasped. Justine's ex-boyfriend, she thought. The one she dumped for Slash. Whoever Slash was. "Did you talk to him?"

"Yeah. He told me some very interesting stuff," Debra replied. "He said that he and Justine used to be close. *Very* close. But the months before she died, she did a complete one-eighty. Turnaround city."

"*And . . .*"

"She never called him. She never had time for any of her old friends. She never hung out. She'd brush past Eddie at school as if she never saw him."

Clarissa remembered the diary. "That sounds about right."

"And then he told me something weird. He said . . ."

"What?" Clarissa pleaded. "Tell me!"

"Hold on a sec," Debra replied. "I think I hear something."

A few moments passed. "Deb? Are you there?" Clarissa asked into the phone.

A door slammed on the other end of the line. "*You!*" she heard Debra whisper harshly. "I had a feeling. . . ."

"Deb?" Clarissa asked again.

"No!" she heard Debra cry. "Get away from me!"

A sharp *bang* made Clarissa jump. It sounded like Debra's phone hitting the floor.

Clarissa heard a sharp scream. The scream cut off abruptly.

"Deb? Deb?" Clarissa shrieked into the phone.

Silence.

Then Clarissa heard a *click*.

Someone hung up the phone.

Chapter Thirteen

C larissa held the phone until the dial tone rang in her ear. It's a joke, she told herself. Debra's just playing around. I'll call her back, and she'll answer the phone and laugh.

Right?

She gripped the phone tightly, and hit redial.

The phone rang and rang and rang. Finally the answering machine picked up.

Clarissa hung up and charged downstairs.

Not a joke. Not a joke. Not a joke. Debra's in trouble.

Justine warned us, Clarissa thought.

Got to get to Deb's . . . before it's too late.

The Lakes didn't live far—over on Melinda Lane. By the time Clarissa reached the front door, her chest was burning. She struggled to breathe. Her heart thundered in her ears.

She rang the doorbell. "Deb!" Clarissa gasped.

No answer.

No one home. No one.

No time to call the police. I have to get inside—now!

She crouched into the side bushes. There. Taped to a branch. The spare key. She'd seen Debra use it a hundred times.

Her hands shook as she turned the key in the lock. The door clicked open.

"Deb! Where are you?" Clarissa called out. She sprinted through the foyer and into the kitchen.

No one there.

The phone sat in its cradle, as if nothing were wrong. Clarissa picked it up and heard a dial tone, just like normal.

She hung it back up.

She found a burrito on a plate with two bites taken out of it. Debra's favorite food.

"Debra?" she called out again.

No reply.

Clarissa left the kitchen and hurried to the stairs.

She stopped with a horrified gasp.

Debra lay sprawled at the foot of the steps. Her left ankle was caught in the wooden spokes of the banister, twisted and red. Her arms were flung wide. Her body lay limp and still.

One eye had rolled back to white. The other stared out at nothing.

Blood from her head dripped down her face.

Into her open mouth.

Wet and glistening.

Debra is dead, Clarissa saw, dropping to her knees.

Debra is dead.

"So far," Detective Larson said, sitting at his desk, "we don't see any reason to think that Debra Lake was murdered."

Clarissa's heart sank.

She'd spent nearly all of Thursday morning and afternoon at the police station, in this cramped office. All the hours of explaining what she heard over the phone. How she found Debra. It was no use.

The husky detective stared at her from behind a stack of papers on top of his desk. Clarissa could hear his nose whistling with his every breath.

Why does he keep *looking* at me? she wondered. He doesn't believe me. I just know it.

Clarissa cleared her throat. "What about the phone?" she asked hoarsely. "It was hung up. How could it be hung up if she's dead? Someone else had to do it."

Larson nodded. "You said yourself that you hung it up after you called 911. Your prints were on the phone. So were Debra's and all of her family's. But that's it. She wasn't paying attention to her footing, and she fell down the stairs. Her death was an accident."

"It wasn't an accident," Clarissa insisted. "Deb was murdered. I know it."

"You've had a shock, Clarissa," the officer replied. "*Two* shocks. Miss Lake's and your sister's deaths were very similar. It's natural for you to think that they're linked in some way. But we've investigated a lot of murders in Shadyside, and we don't see any evidence of foul play. I'm sorry."

"So I'm *lying*?" she asked, glaring at him.

"No, I don't think so," Detective Larson replied. "I think you heard your friend fall down the stairs. But your imagination is filling in the blanks."

"But the phone—"

"*You* hung up the phone, Clarissa."

"And when I heard Debra say, 'Get away from me'?"

"Maybe she said it and maybe she didn't. As I said, your mind can play tricks on you."

Clarissa sighed and slumped deeper into her seat. He'll never believe me, she told herself.

Then she had an idea. Why didn't I think

of this before? We could call Renata.

"Detective Larson," Clarissa sat up straight. "I have someone who will vouch for my story. Someone who knows my sister was murdered. And knows that Deb was killed, too."

Detective Larson raised his eyebrows.

"Renata," Clarissa announced. "She's a psychic. Justine used to call her all the time. And then when I called, Justine spoke to me through Renata. Told me she was murdered. Warned me that someone else was going to die."

"Clarissa," Detective Larson shook his head. "I don't think—"

"Please!" Clarissa pleaded. "Just talk to Renata. She knows what's going on. She'll tell you I didn't imagine any of this!"

The detective reluctantly picked up the phone, and Clarissa recited the number from memory. A few moments later, Detective Larson was speaking with Renata.

"Uh-huh. I see," the detective said into the phone. "Thank you for your time." Then he hung up.

"Well?" Clarissa asked. "What did she say?"

Larson leaned back in his chair and folded his arms across his large chest. His deep-set eyes focused on her. "She claims she's never heard of you *or* your sister."

Chapter Fourteen

C larissa's jaw dropped open. "She's lying! Call her back. Let me talk to her. Please!"

Larson leaned forward. "Let me tell you something, Clarissa." His voice became lower and more earnest. "I know about your . . . troubles. And I know you've spent time in the clinic."

Clarissa felt her temperature rise with every word he uttered. She wanted to explode. She wanted to shake him until he believed her. "It's true!" she cried. "I'm not making this up!"

"For your own good," Larson suggested, "don't mention the psychic again."

"I know it's hard to believe, Detective Larson, but . . . " Clarissa let her voice trail off. What's the use? she thought. "Never mind," she muttered. "Can I go now?"

Detective Larson nodded.

Clarissa met her parents outside the detective's office. They made their way to the car without a word.

Clarissa stared blankly out the window on the ride back to Fear Street. Justine *warned* me, Clarissa thought. I should have told Debra in person. I shouldn't have called her.

Then maybe she'd still be alive.

Clarissa closed her eyes as the car swung into their driveway. She couldn't think about it anymore.

Mira and Aaron were waiting on the front porch.

Clarissa climbed out of the car and trudged up the walk to the steps.

Mira ran to Clarissa and hugged her. "Debra's gone! Deb's really gone!" she cried. "I can't believe it!"

"The cops won't do anything," Clarissa mumbled. "They think it was an accident."

"Did something bad happen?" came a small voice.

Aaron. He stared up at Clarissa with his big brown eyes, holding Oscar in his arms.

"Yes," she replied. "Something very bad."

Aaron hugged the stuffed animal a little tighter.

"Let's all go inside," Mr. Turner suggested. "We'll get some dinner going." He glanced at Clarissa. "Maybe you should go upstairs and lie down."

Clarissa trudged up the stairs to Justine's room. But not to rest. She had something to do . . . something she'd been dying to do all day.

Debra had started to tell Clarissa something right before she was killed. Something that Eddie Robbins had said.

Clarissa told Detective Larson this. He didn't seem to care.

But Clarissa did.

She had to call Eddie. Had to know what he said to Debra.

She went straight to the closet and opened it. On the inside of the door, Justine had written dozens of phone numbers. It had made her father furious, but Justine did it anyway. She thought it was cooler than a little black book. There were numbers for most of her friends, the movie theater, Pete's Pizza.

She didn't see Slash's name.

But Hammerhead was on the list. Eddie.

Clarissa dialed his number.

Eddie answered.

"Hi, Eddie. It's Clarissa Turner."

Eddie sighed. "Hi." His voice was deep and tired. As if he'd been sleeping. "I heard about Debra Lake. Jason Klein told me."

Jason? Clarissa wondered. Oh. Kenny Klein's older brother.

"I can't believe it," Eddie went on. "I mean, I saw her at the mall yesterday. Then two hours later she's dead. It's so weird."

"I know," Clarissa replied. "She told me she saw you. I . . . I was the one on the phone with her when she died."

Eddie didn't answer right away.

"I know how that feels," he said after a moment.

Clarissa knew he must be remembering the moment when Justine died. When *he* was on the other end of the line.

"I'm calling about—"

"I miss her."

Clarissa paused. "Huh?"

"Justine. I miss her."

Clarissa closed her eyes and sank onto the bed. "I know. So do I."

"It wasn't right. The way she died."

Clarissa wanted to tell him how her sister really died. But she didn't dare. Not when the police didn't believe her.

"Eddie, I'm calling about Deb. She was about to tell me something before she died. Something you told her at the mall."

Eddie cleared his throat. "I told her how Justine had changed."

"I know," she replied. "But this was something that Deb said was really important."

"I don't know. . . ."

"Try to remember, Eddie. Please."

"Are you sure you want to know, Clarissa? Deb was pretty freaked when I told her. She said she wasn't sure she'd even tell you."

Clarissa's heart was racing. Debra had said it was important. That it involved Justine. "You *have* to tell me, Eddie," she pleaded. "You have to!"

She heard Eddie clear his throat again. "You know that we broke up because Justine was going out with another guy, right?" he asked.

"Uh-huh," Clarissa said. She'd read it in Justine's diary. Her sister was seeing Slash.

"Well . . . you know the guy you're going with," Eddie continued. "Will Reynolds?"

"Uh, *yes*," she said.

"He's the guy Justine was seeing," Eddie said.

Chapter Fifteen

Clarissa's body went numb. She could hardly feel the phone in her hand. She had to force the words out. "Justine . . . and *Will*?"

"Sorry, Clarissa," Eddie said softly.

"But . . . why didn't *Will* tell me?" she asked.

"I don't know."

Clarissa thought about the diary.

About Slash.

His jealousy. How he pushed Justine. Started stalking her.

Could it be true? she wondered.

Could Will be Slash?

Clarissa had to ask Eddie one more question. "Have you ever heard the name Slash?" she asked.

Eddie was silent a moment. "No. Why?"

"I found out that Justine was seeing some guy named Slash," Clarissa replied. "Do you think it might be Will?"

"Could be," Eddie murmured. "But I really don't know."

Clarissa sighed. "Thanks, Eddie."

They hung up.

Clarissa paced the room. She picked the hunting knife up off the desk and ran her fingers over the leather cover. *SLASH*.

It made sense. Justine was into music, just like Will. He prowled those clubs in Center City. Why *wouldn't* they hit it off? Smiling, dancing . . . kissing.

The very thought of Will and Justine together . . . it changed everything. Will was Clarissa's first boyfriend. She thought that he liked her for *her*. But what if he started going with Clarissa because she reminded him of Justine?

Clarissa felt sick to her stomach.

Her mother called her down to dinner. But Clarissa didn't want to eat. She called Mira instead. Told her what Eddie had said.

"I'll be right over," Mira promised.

When she arrived, Clarissa locked the bedroom door. Mira's mouth dropped when she saw Clarissa. "How long have you been crying?"

"Just a little while," Clarissa replied. "It's not every day my best friend gets killed, *and*

I find out my boyfriend was obsessed with my sister."

"Are you sure that Will and Justine were . . . together?" Mira asked.

"That's what we're going to ask Renata. And Justine. The diary said that this guy Slash was obsessed with her. He sent her a dead bird in the mail. He's a total psycho."

Clarissa showed Mira the hunting knife. Mira's eyes widened. "Whoa. This thing is sharp." She shook her head. "Do you really think Slash could be Will?"

"I can't think of any other explanation," Clarissa replied.

"I don't know," Mira said. "I've known Will for two years. He might have a temper, but I've never seen him hurt a fly. He can't be Slash."

"Who else, then?" Clarissa murmured, tears streaming down her face again. "It's the only thing that makes sense."

"Listen to me, Clarissa," Mira insisted. "Even if he was Slash, Will couldn't do this. He's not a killer. I know it."

Clarissa stared deep into her eyes. "How?"

Mira shrugged. "I don't know how. I just know."

But she wouldn't meet Clarissa's gaze. Mira's not sure, Clarissa thought.

Clarissa picked up the cordless phone. "I'm calling Renata," she said, and dialed the number. Renata answered on the second ring.

"It's Clarissa Turner."

"I know who you are," Renata replied gruffly.

"Then why did you tell the police that you didn't?"

Renata sighed. "I'm sorry, Clarissa. About that and about your friend. But I couldn't tell them I knew you. Most cops don't believe psychics. I just can't afford to get involved with the police."

"That's all you have to say?" Mira cried shrilly. "Our friend is dead. If you would have backed Clarissa up, Detective Larson might have believed that she was murdered."

"No, he wouldn't," Renata replied sternly. "Clarissa, you saw their reactions, right?"

"Renata, I have more questions for my sister," Clarissa pleaded.

"I know," Renata replied wearily. "But I can't help you today. I'm resting from another call. I'm sorry."

The line went dead.

"Renata? *Renata!* I don't believe it! She hung up on me!" Clarissa put her finger on Redial. "I'm calling her back."

"She's not going to help us," Mira said bitterly. "Why bother?"

Clarissa glared at Mira. "What else can we do? I mean, Will probably killed Justine and

Debra. And—"

Mira sank back onto the bed. "Just because he lied to you about seeing Justine doesn't make him a killer," Mira said. "If you want . . . " Mira paused. "No, forget it."

Clarissa sat up. "What?"

"Nothing."

"Come on, Mira. Tell me."

"Well . . . " Mira began. "I can talk to Will. Sort of ask him where he was last night when Debra died. He might talk to me."

"No," Clarissa said. "It's too dangerous. And he'd never tell you if he killed Debra."

"No, but he might have a real alibi," Mira replied. "And I don't have to talk to him in person. I can ask him by e-mail."

Clarissa thought about it. "I guess that's okay. If you only e-mail him."

"We can do it right now," Mira said, pointing to Clarissa's computer. "Are you online?"

Clarissa nodded. She turned on the computer.

Mira accessed her e-mail account, then typed:

WILL, I SAW DAVE AND FREDERICK FROM YOUR BAND LAST NIGHT IN CENTER CITY. WHERE WERE YOU?

Mira turned to Clarissa. "That's it. We'll see what he says." Mira checked her watch. "I have to go. My mom wants me home for dinner tonight." She put a hand on Clarissa's shoulder. "Are you going to be all right?"

Clarissa nodded. "Be careful, okay?"

"I will," Mira said, grabbing her bag. "And I'll call you when I hear something."

Clarissa stretched out on her bed and tried to relax. But she couldn't. All she kept picturing was Will and Justine together.

She stared at the knife.

SLASH.

Maybe he *was* somewhere else last night.

Or maybe he'll lie about that, too, Clarissa thought. She wiped away a tear and rolled over. Mira's plan didn't seem too promising.

Her eyelids gradually closed. She felt so tired.

The phone rang.

Clarissa jumped, startled out of her drowsiness. She picked up the receiver. "Hello?"

Crackling static echoed through the receiver. "Hello?" she repeated.

She stood up and moved to the bedroom door. I must have fallen asleep, she thought. What time is it? Are my parents awake?

More static.

"Is anyone there?" Clarissa asked into the phone. She gazed down the hallway. Moonlight glowed through the window again, just as it had when Justine's ghost appeared.

A surge of excitement passed through her. Could Justine be trying to reach me?

The static crackled on the phone.

"Who is this?" she demanded.

Then she saw something. At the end of the hall by the stairs. A fluttering of . . .

Clarissa crept down the hall, still holding the phone to her ear.

"Justine?" she whispered. "Is it you?"

She reached the steps. Everything around her glowed silver from the moonlight. She peered down the stairs.

More static in the phone receiver.

"Justine?"

Clarissa heard something behind her. A creaking floorboard.

"Who—"

Two hands slammed into her back. Clarissa flew forward. She reached out with her free hand, but grasped nothing!

Her stomach lurched.

She fell.

Fell down the stairs.

The phone spun out of her hands and rolled underneath her.

Her head slammed onto a step.

Her body twisted.

Clarissa heard something *snap*.

An unbearable pain shot through her neck. Hold on, Clarissa thought. But she couldn't stop herself.

She flopped down the remaining steps, her arms and legs limp. Then she came to rest at the bottom.

The pain ended. Clarissa couldn't move.

She lay helpless. On her stomach. At the foot of the stairs.

But she could see the ceiling. Her head had twisted completely around on her neck!

I'm dying, Clarissa thought.

Just like my sister.

larissa woke up with a start. Sweat beaded on her forehead.

It wasn't real. I'm alive. On my bed. In my room.

When did I turn the lights out? she wondered.

Clarissa shook her head. Then she rolled over.

And gasped.

Will stood over her bed.

Watching her.

He clamped a hand over her mouth. "Don't scream."

Clarissa couldn't move. Her whole body trembled. This is it, she thought. First Justine, then Debra, and now me.

"Promise you won't scream?" Will raised a finger to his lips.

Clarissa nodded. He pulled his hand away.

"I'm sorry I scared you," he whispered. "But I didn't want to have to deal with your parents. So I took the shortcut." He gestured to the open window.

Outside, night had fallen. How long had she slept?

Her clock read 8:30.

Mom and Dad are probably still downstairs.

"What are you doing here, Will?" Clarissa asked in a whisper.

"I heard about Debra," he replied. "I thought you might want company."

"Company?" She sat up on her bed.

"Yeah." He ran a finger across Clarissa's cheek.

She cringed.

"You've been crying. I can tell. I wanted to be here for you." He glanced at her. "Is that *bad*?"

"No," Clarissa replied. "But you know what *is* bad?"

Will seemed puzzled. "What?"

"Lying to my *face*," Clarissa said. "*Slash*."

Will closed his eyes. He didn't reply.

"You were Justine's secret boyfriend," Clarissa said through gritted teeth. "You were the one she ditched school for. And you never told me. Even when I showed you the diary."

"Who told you?" he growled, his face turning in anger.

Clarissa stared at him defiantly. She didn't want him to know that Eddie Robbins had helped her. She didn't want Will to go after him. "Justine," she lied.

"Oh, yeah," he said sarcastically. "I forgot. She's been calling you from the other side."

"But you admit it?" Clarissa asked. "You went with Justine?"

Will nodded slowly.

Clarissa crept back on her bed. Her back hit the headboard. "Then you did it?"

"Huh? Did what?" Will asked.

Killed my sister, Clarissa said to herself. She wanted Will to admit to it on his own. "Come on, you know what I'm talking about," she choked out. "You didn't think I'd figure it out, did you?"

Will shook his head. "I'm so sorry." He inched closer to Clarissa. "I never meant to hurt Justine. . . . You believe me, don't you?"

Clarissa gasped. He *did* do it. He killed my sister and my best friend!

Clarissa didn't know what to say next. A murderer is in my room, she thought, shivering. He's sitting on my bed. Just inches away from me!

She pushed herself harder against the

headboard. "M-maybe you should go," she told him.

"I said I was sorry, Clarissa." Will leaned in a little closer. "What more can I do?" He gently stroked Clarissa's hair. "We just have to forget about it and move on, okay?"

Clarissa's face grew hot. Was he asking her to forget about her *sister*? And forget about her *best friend*?

"Move *on*?" she cried out. "You *killed* them!"

Will's eyes opened wide. "Excuse me? Wait a minute. I—"

"You knew that Deb was going to tell me about you and Justine. You were right behind her. You pushed her down the stairs."

"I can't believe this!" he cried.

"And Justine. She broke up with you, just as the diary said. And you couldn't take it. *Right*?"

"Clarissa . . . "

"You couldn't have her, so you made sure no one could. You murdered my sister!"

"*No!*" Will cried.

Clarissa glanced at the bedroom door. Did her parents hear him?

Will must have wondered the same thing, because he lowered his voice to a growl.

"I was with your sister," he whispered. "And she ripped my heart out when she dumped me. I did some things I shouldn't have." He swallowed hard. "I . . . I got so jealous."

"So you *stalked* her?" Clarissa probed. "And sent her a dead bird?"

"I was a little over the edge." He glared at her. "But I got over it. Hear me? I got over it. I didn't kill her. I'm not a murderer."

Clarissa didn't answer.

"And as for Debra," he continued, "that's just crazy. I was in Center City last night. I couldn't have killed her if I wanted to. And I *didn't* want to."

Clarissa wiped her eyes. She wasn't going to lose it in front of Will. She had to be strong. Make him think she wasn't afraid. Get him out of there.

"And I'm supposed to believe that?" Clarissa sneered. "You're a liar. You'd never tell the truth if it meant getting caught."

Will sighed. "I should've told you about us from the beginning, I know. But at her funeral . . . I saw you standing there crying. And you reminded me of her so much. I knew then I had to meet you."

He took a deep breath. "And when I did, I found out that you weren't anything like your sister. You were *you*. And it was so great when we hung out. . . . I couldn't bring myself to tell you. I didn't want to ruin it between us, Clarissa. You *have* to believe me."

Clarissa didn't know what to think. Her head spun. She felt so confused. But she had to be careful. He was a good liar. Such a good liar.

"No," she said finally, shaking her head and moving to the other side of the bed. "Renata—"

"No one believes you," he interrupted her. "You think if you tell the police your dead sister told you I'm a murderer, they're going to believe you? Get real."

Will leaned closer to Clarissa, inches from her face. "That woman filled your head with garbage."

"Get out of here," Clarissa growled. "Right now. And don't even think of coming near me or Mira again."

Will's eyes were moist and wide in their sockets. His lower lip quivered.

"You're . . . *dumping* me," he whispered. "Just like your sister."

"Get out, Will."

"I can't believe it." He slowly rose to his feet. "You're *crazy*. . . . Justine is *dead*, Clarissa. *Accept* it."

"I told you to get *out!*" Clarissa cried.

He leveled a finger at her. "You should go back to the clinic where you belong!"

"Get *out!*" she roared. "*GET OUT GET OUT GET OUT!*"

Clarissa heard a door swing open down

the hall. My parents, she thought.

Will heard it, too. He crossed to the window and stuck one leg over the sill. "You'll regret this, Clarissa," he said. "You'll regret it until the day you die."

Chapter Seventeen

Will slipped out the window.
Seconds later the bedroom doorknob rattled. A fist banged on the
door. "Clarissa!" her father bellowed.

The door flew open. Her father flicked on
the light.

"What's going on up here?" he demanded.
"Who were you screaming at?"

"Will," she muttered, choking back the
tears. "He came in through the window while
I was sleeping."

Her father crossed the room and peered
out into the night. He shut the window and
locked it. "So how long has this been going
on?" he asked. "How long has Will been
sneaking into your room?"

Clarissa's mother entered the room. "What happened?" she asked.

"Clarissa was just about to tell me," her father replied, folding his arms.

Clarissa shivered, remembering Will's threat. She knew if she didn't tell her parents everything, they wouldn't be able to help her.

And Will *would* be back.

"I found out a lot of things," Clarissa began. She told them about Justine sneaking out to go to Center City with a boy.

"What?" her mother cried. "I never knew."

Clarissa nodded. "And . . . Will was the boy she was seeing," she explained. "I just found out. That's what Debra was trying to tell me before she was pushed down the stairs."

"She wasn't pushed, honey—" her father began.

"Yes, she *was*!" Clarissa protested. "Why is it so hard for everyone to believe? I *heard* it! Justine warned us about it! She said one of us was going to die! And she was *right*!"

Clarissa's mother eased herself down on the edge of the bed and glanced at Clarissa's father. Clarissa knew that look. *The Clarissa-is-still-confused* look.

"Detective Larson mentioned this," her father said slowly. "He said you told him about a psychic."

"Renata," Clarissa murmured.

"So you're still *talking* with Justine?" her father asked.

Clarissa couldn't hold back the truth. Not anymore. "Yes," she replied.

"Through that . . . psychic?" her mother asked.

"Yes," Clarissa said again. "I spoke to her a few hours ago. Right on this phone."

Clarissa held up the cordless phone.

Her parents shared another glance.

"*That* phone?" her mother asked.

Clarissa nodded.

"Impossible," her father declared.

"Why?" Clarissa asked. "I picked up the phone, I pressed the button, and I dialed. What's the big deal?"

"Honey," Clarissa's mother said softly. "You couldn't have spoken to *anyone* on that phone. It's been disconnected since Justine's funeral. The line is *dead*."

Chapter Eighteen

"Dead? No! Justine's phone *can't* be dead!" Clarissa cried shrilly. "I just used it!"

"Let me see it." Her father held out his hand.

She gave him the phone. He punched the On button and listened. He gazed at Clarissa and handed back the phone.

Clarissa held the phone to her ear. No dial tone. Nothing.

"It can't be," she mumbled. She hit the On button again. Still no dial tone. "It was working before. I swear!"

Her dad pulled the phone from her hand and reset it in its cradle. He disconnected the cord from the wall jack and wrapped up the whole unit.

"What are you doing?" Clarissa cried. "You can't take it!"

"We'll make sure you get a session with Dr. Sayles," her dad said softly, holding the phone under his arm. "I want you to tell him everything that's happened the last few days. Then we'll decide where to go from there."

Clarissa's eyes filled with tears. "Please don't take the phone away, Dad. Please!"

"We're doing the right thing," her mother said. She reached out and squeezed Clarissa's hand.

Clarissa could barely see her mother's face through the tears. "I'm not crazy, Mom. You have to believe me."

"Nobody said you were crazy." Her mother kissed her forehead. "You're a little confused. But everything will sort itself out."

"Confused," Clarissa whispered.

"You've been through so much," her mother added. "It's no surprise that you're having a little trouble. I just couldn't see it. I've been so upset. . . . "

"It's for the best," her father said. "And don't worry. I'll deal with Will."

Clarissa slumped back down on the bed. She wiped her eyes.

"Everything will be fine," her mother promised. "You'll see."

"I hope you're right," Clarissa replied, and tried to smile.

But I know you're wrong, she thought. Will is going to come back. And he's going to try to kill me.

The next day Clarissa cut school. She didn't want to run into Will. That afternoon she caught up with Mira outside of Pete's Pizza.

They walked home together. The air was crisp, just cold enough to hint at the winter to come. Clarissa pulled her jacket closer. She told Mira all about Will's visit.

Mira shook her head. "Then he did kill Justine and Debra."

"He swore he didn't. But he was lying. What are we going to do?" Clarissa demanded.

"We have to stick together," Mira said, putting an arm around Clarissa. "If we stick together, we'll be okay."

"Why don't you stay at my house tonight," Clarissa suggested.

"Good idea," Mira said. "I just have to get some stuff from home. Maybe we should call Renata. Talk to Justine about this."

Clarissa shoved her hands in her coat pockets. "We can't. My parents took away the phone."

"Why?" Mira asked.

"I was stupid," she told her. "I told them I'd been calling Renata on that phone."

"You're right," Mira said. "That *was* stupid."

Clarissa sighed. "The weird thing is my dad said the phone line was disconnected."

Mira blinked. "Huh? How did the phone work for us?"

"No idea," Clarissa replied. "We both *know* it worked. Now how are we going to talk to Renata?" Clarissa asked. "I can't call from the phone in my kitchen. If my parents heard me, they'd go berserk."

"There's a pay phone on the corner," Mira suggested. "Try it. You can charge it to my calling card."

Clarissa lifted the receiver and dialed Renata's number from memory.

It rang and rang.

"Come *on*," Clarissa pleaded. "Pick up!"

"Clarissa?" Renata asked just as she was about to hang up.

"Yes."

"I knew I'd be hearing from you. Have the police changed their minds?"

"No way."

"Of course not. You need to talk to Justine, then?"

"Yes. Can you do it?"

"I'll try," Renata said.

The psychic began her chants. Clarissa nibbled a fingernail and gazed hopefully at Mira.

But instead of hearing the heavy breathing, the chanting grew louder. Then it changed into furious barking sounds.

"What's going on?" Mira asked.

Clarissa shrugged.

Finally, Renata groaned. "It's no good," she declared wearily. "No use."

"What is it?" Clarissa demanded. "What's wrong?"

"I can't find her," Renata croaked. "Justine is . . . gone!"

Chapter Nineteen

"I can't sense her." Renata drew a deep breath and cleared her throat. "No. It was so strong before. But now there's nothing."

"How can that be?" Clarissa argued. "Where did she go?"

"I'm not sure," Renata replied. "Everything feels totally different now. It's almost as if . . . " She paused. "Are you calling from a different place?"

"Yes. We're at a pay phone," Clarissa replied.

"And the other calls?"

"I made them all from my . . . from Justine's old bedroom," Clarissa replied. "But my dad took Justine's phone away from me. He said the line was dead."

"If Justine was talking on that phone when she died," Renata said slowly, "part of her essence might have bonded to it."

"What does that mean?" Clarissa asked.

"The spirits need a link to contact our world," Renata explained. "It could be a piece of clothing, a flower, a memory. In this case, Justine's spirit connected with her phone. Probably the very instant she died." Renata paused. "You have to get that phone back, Clarissa. It's crucial."

Clarissa sighed in frustration. "Okay. I'll try."

"Good luck," Renata said, and hung up.

Clarissa turned to Mira. "We have to get that phone."

Mira nodded. "I'll meet you at your house."

"Right," Clarissa said, and headed home.

Clarissa turned the doorknob to her father's study. "This is the last place to look," she told Mira.

They had waited until everyone went to sleep to search for Justine's phone. But they didn't find it.

"Turn on a light," Mira suggested as they sneaked in.

"No," Clarissa argued. "They might notice it."

"How are we going to find anything in

here?" Mira grumbled. "It's pitch black."

"It's probably by the desk," Clarissa said. "I know my way."

Clarissa crept around her father's desk. She carefully rolled his chair back and crouched by a set of drawers. She opened one.

Pens, notepads, paper clips, staples. No phone.

Nothing in the next drawer, either.

The third drawer was locked.

"Do you think it's in there?" Mira whispered.

"We'll soon find out." Clarissa grabbed a paper clip, untwisted it, and jiggled it in the lock. When she heard a *click* she pulled open the drawer.

Nothing but files.

Clarissa moved to the set of drawers on the other side of the desk.

No phone.

"Where'd he put it?" she asked.

A board in the ceiling creaked.

Then Clarissa heard footsteps.

"We're nailed!" Mira whispered.

"Quick! Into the kitchen!"

Clarissa carefully shut the last drawer and slid around the side of the desk. As she did, she caught sight of something on top of her father's file cabinet.

The phone!

Clarissa grabbed it.

"Here." She shoved it into Mira's hands. "Run to the bathroom. He won't see you!"

"Clar—"

"*Go!*"

Mira scooted across to the kitchen, jammed her toe on a chair leg, and hobbled into the bathroom on the other side.

Clarissa eased the study door closed with a click. Then she ran to the kitchen and opened the refrigerator.

"You girls still awake?" Her father yawned as he plodded over to the sink.

"Yeah," Clarissa replied, pulling out some leftover chicken. "There's a late movie on."

"Not *too* late," Mr. Turner mumbled. He poured himself a glass of water and chugged it down. "Night."

"Night, Dad."

Mira slipped out of the bathroom after he left. She plopped down in a chair and rubbed her foot.

"I think I broke my little toe," she grumbled.

"Sorry," Clarissa replied, picking up the phone. "But we got it!"

They climbed the stairs to Clarissa's room. "I hope this is all over soon," she murmured as she shut and locked the door. "I can't take much more of this."

She plugged the phone into the wall. Then she dialed Renata's number.

It rang.

Ten times. Fifteen.

"Maybe it's too late," Mira said. "It's pushing one o'clock."

Clarissa sighed and hung up. "Now what? Should we just crash?"

Mira yawned. "Yeah. Guess so. Nothing else we can do tonight."

"Okay," Clarissa said. She checked the lock on the window.

"Better hide the phone," Mira added. "Your father will see it on the nightstand."

Clarissa nodded and wrapped the cord around the phone. She opened the closet door and lifted the loose floorboard where she had found the diary and knife. She hid the phone there.

They climbed into their beds and shut the light. Clarissa was exhausted, but still she couldn't sleep. She couldn't stop thinking about Justine and Debra . . . and Will.

It was going to be a long night.

Clarissa woke with a start.

"Get up!" Mira shook her hard.

"Huh?" Clarissa glimpsed the clock through her bleary eyes. 1:37.

"I heard a noise outside," Mira whispered. "I'm scared."

Clarissa strained her ears.

She heard it, too. A *thud*. It sounded as if

something hit the side of the house.

Clarissa froze.

The trellis.

Someone was climbing it.

"It's Will," Mira breathed. "He's here. I know it."

"He can't get in," Clarissa said. "The window's locked."

"No!" Mira cried. "I opened it while you were sleeping. To get some air. I'm not sure if I locked it or not!"

Clarissa's heart stopped. "You're not *sure*? A murderer is out to get us, and you might have left the window *open*?"

"We have to do something," Mira whispered frantically. "We're going to die! He's going to kill us!"

Clarissa jumped off the bed and ran to lock the window.

Too late.

Will was already there. Gazing in at her. His hands sliding open the glass.

"He's coming in!" Mira cried, leaping behind Clarissa.

No time to think.

Clarissa grabbed the hunting knife off her desk.

He killed Justine. He killed Debra. Now he's here to kill us! Clarissa thought.

The knife shook in Clarissa's hand.

Will grinned as he lifted the window open

wide. The night breeze drifted in, mixed with the soft aroma of Will's leather jacket.

Clarissa used to love that leather smell. Now it repulsed her.

Will's smile faded when he saw the knife in her hand. "Look. We can talk about this, right?" He reached in through the window and clamped a hand around Clarissa's arm.

"No!" Clarissa tried to yank free. But his grasp was like a vise. She swatted uselessly at his arm.

Mira began punching Will's shoulder through the window. "Get lost! Get off her!"

Will shook his head violently. "You're making a mistake! I—"

Mira pounded on the hand that gripped the windowsill.

Will growled in pain and started to slip.

"Let . . . go . . . of . . . me!" Clarissa tried to pry his fingers off her arm.

"No! Listen to me!" Will shrieked. He gripped her arm tighter.

Clarissa shoved him in the chest as hard as she could.

Will's fingers flexed wildly. He lost his hold on the windowsill.

His hand slipped off her arm.

Will's mouth opened in horror as he fell back off the trellis.

"Nooooooo!"

He screamed all the way down.

Chapter Twenty

"Hello, Clarissa," Dr. Sayles said cheerfully. "How do you feel this morning?"

Clarissa stared at him and didn't reply.

"I guess you're upset to be back here," the doctor said, his eyes studying her.

"I guess," Clarissa muttered.

At least it's quiet in here, she thought. Saturday had been a day of screaming, angry, emotional voices. Police questions. Questions from her parents. Endless questions and questioning eyes, staring at her, studying her . . .

Everyone thinking, "Poor Clarissa. She's lost it again."

Poor, lost Clarissa.

129

And now she truly *was* lost.

Lost to her friends. Lost to her family. Back in the clinic with this doctor and his false cheerfulness.

They weren't even going to let her go to Debra's funeral.

"How is Will?" she asked the doctor.

"Well, the final tally is in," he replied as he settled into a chair behind his desk. "He has a broken femur, and a shattered wrist. He'll be in the hospital for a while. The police are questioning him thoroughly."

"They are?" Clarissa asked, sitting up.

"Don't get your hopes up," Dr. Sayles said gently. "Will is still denying that he killed anyone."

She slumped back into the sofa. "Of course he is."

"I want you to think about that, Clarissa. I know you don't believe it, but just imagine for a moment that Will is innocent. That Justine and Debra's deaths were accidental, as the police say. How does that make you feel?"

"Angry," she muttered.

Clarissa knew the routine—go along with whatever the doctor said, and she'd get out of this place sooner.

"Clarissa, you're not a sick girl," Dr. Sayles explained, stroking his gray beard. "But you have a very powerful imagination. The deaths hurt you very deeply. You *needed* to believe that there was a reason for the deaths."

Clarissa agreed with Dr. Sayles. She didn't fight. She knew the more she fought, the longer she would be in the clinic. They would eventually name a wing after her.

"The first step in your recovery is to apologize to Will. You have to talk to him," he said, dialing the phone. "Face your fears head on."

Dr. Sayles cleared his throat. "Uh, yes, Will Reynolds's room," he said into the receiver. Then he held it out to Clarissa.

"What?" Clarissa shot her body upright. "Here? Now?"

"You want to get out of here as soon as possible," Dr. Sayles replied. "Right?"

Clarissa heaved herself off the couch and grabbed the phone. She couldn't believe Dr. Sayles was making her do this.

Will answered the phone. "Hello?"

"Uh, hi, Will," she stammered. "It's Clarissa."

"Clarissa?"

"I'm just calling to apologize for pushing you out of my window." Clarissa glanced at Dr. Sayles. "It's part of my therapy."

"Don't worry about it," Will said. "I'll be okay. I know Mira scared you into doing it."

"No. She—"

Will cut her off. "Clarissa . . . I think I

believe you now. About Justine. About everything."

"You do?" Clarissa asked softly.

"Look," Will said. "I have to tell you something about Mira. Something that I should have told you a long time ago."

"What is it?" Clarissa asked.

"Mira likes me. She's been after me since before I met Justine. I didn't want to say anything because the two of you are friends. I thought Mira would get the hint. But she didn't."

Will cleared his throat.

"And the more I think about it . . . she made hints. She said things about Justine's death. I never put it together before. Maybe . . . maybe I'd better talk to the police about Mira."

"No way," Clarissa murmured. Mira believed her from the beginning. And Mira was the one who was there for Clarissa.

How could he say this about Mira? It couldn't be true. Mira was Clarissa's best friend.

Did Will *really* mean it when he said he believed her? she wondered. Was he really going to talk to the police, or was he just saying that?

Will lied to me, Clarissa thought. He betrayed me. He's probably making this up to protect himself.

"I *know* what you're trying to do," Clarissa told him. "You're trying to confuse me."

"You have to believe me," Will pleaded. "I think you're in danger!"

"There's no way I'm going to believe *you*!" she screamed into the phone. "Never! Never! Never!"

Clarissa slammed the receiver into its cradle. Then she turned to Dr. Sayles. "Um . . . that went well," she said sarcastically.

He shook his head. "I think that's enough for today. You'd better go to your room now and rest."

"I blew it," Clarissa muttered as she made her way back to her room. "I'm going to be in here for months."

Later that afternoon Clarissa's parents came to visit. They brought along Aaron and Mira.

"Mira offered to watch Aaron for us," her mother explained. "We're going to do some shopping later."

"Don't get too attached to Mira," Clarissa teased Aaron, ruffling his hair. "I'll be home soon."

The visit was pretty much like the ones Clarissa remembered from her last stay at the clinic. They sat in the TV room for a while discussing her sessions, her progress, how great it would be when she came home.

It made Clarissa even more homesick.

Finally her parents stood to go. They had to run errands before it got too late.

"You're sure you don't mind watching Aaron?" Mrs. Turner asked Mira.

"No way," Mira replied. "Go. Do your thing. He's in good hands."

Clarissa hugged her parents goodbye, then slumped back into her chair.

"I called the police again," Mira whispered after they left. "I tried to make them believe. I really tried."

Clarissa smiled. "I know, Mira. It's not your fault." She turned her attention to Aaron. "How've you been, big guy?"

"I want you to come home," he replied glumly. "I don't have anyone to play Crazy Eights with."

"You don't?" Clarissa asked. "What about Mira?"

Aaron grinned. "She cheats."

Mira's eyes opened wide and she gasped. "I do not!"

She tickled Aaron's ribs and he giggled. Clarissa joined in. He giggled even harder.

Rrrriiing!

Aaron gazed at Mira's backpack. "It's coming from there."

"My cell phone," Mira explained.

It rang again.

"Cool!" Aaron exclaimed. He zipped open Mira's backpack.

"Hey," Mira cried, lunging toward Aaron. "Get out of there."

"I want to answer the phone!" Aaron declared, quickly pulling it out of the bag.

Clarissa gasped when she saw what was in her brother's hand.

Not Mira's cellular.

Justine's phone.

Chapter Twenty-one

C larissa stared at the phone.

Not hooked up to anything.

It rang again.

Before Clarissa could stop him, Aaron answered it.

Immediately his body lurched. He gazed at Clarissa with glassy eyes. His mouth opened, but nothing came out.

Then a tiny whisper. "*Believe . . . it.*"

Aaron collapsed onto Clarissa's lap.

Mira snatched the phone away from Aaron and raised it to her ear. "Hello? Hello?"

She handed it to Clarissa. "Nothing."

Aaron moaned and opened his eyes. Then he stood up as if nothing had happened. "I have to go to the bathroom," he said. He trotted to the men's room across the hall.

"What was that?" Mira asked. "Is he okay?"

"That was Justine!" Clarissa whispered.

"So now the spirits talk through your little adopted *brother*?" Mira asked. "This is so weird."

"He did it right before Debra died, too," Clarissa said. "Justine needed to contact us. To warn us. What could it mean?"

Clarissa stood up and began to pace the room, her mind whirring. Then she stopped. "What's Justine's phone doing in your pack?"

Mira moved closer to Clarissa. "That phone is our only link to Justine," she said, wrapping an arm around Clarissa's shoulders. "I thought I'd keep it at my house so your father couldn't take it again. And I had a chance to snag it today, so . . ."

Clarissa nodded. "Good idea."

Aaron trotted back from the bathroom. "Ice cream, Mira. You promised."

Mira smiled. "I didn't forget. We can go."

"Wait," Clarissa said. She had a weird feeling. Something wasn't right. But she couldn't put her finger on it. "Never mind. Thanks for taking care of Aaron," she told Mira. "That's really nice of you."

Mira squeezed her arm. "Hey. Are you going to be all right?"

"As all right as I can be in here," Clarissa said, trying to sound cheerful for Aaron's sake.

Aaron and Mira said goodbye. Clarissa stared after them until the door to the TV room clicked shut and they were gone.

Then she trekked back to her room and flopped on the bed. She stared at the ceiling.

"Believe it," she repeated in a whisper. "Believe it."

Believe *what*?

Chapter Twenty-two

C larissa couldn't stop thinking about it. She had to get it straight.

Believe *what*?

Was Justine trying to warn her about Will?

Or about Mira?

Should she believe what Will said about Mira?

She swallowed hard. Her best friend—a killer?

Clarissa shook her head. If Mira liked Will so much, why did she help Clarissa push him out the window?

Clarissa couldn't answer that.

A cold shiver ran down Clarissa's spine. Renata had said that the phone was the only connection they had to Justine. Mira said she took it to keep it safe.

But if Mira killed Justine she'd want to get rid of it. To destroy the last link to Justine's spirit.

But the phone *wasn't* the last link.

Aaron had a connection, too.

And Mira saw that when Aaron channeled Justine.

Is Aaron in trouble now? Clarissa wondered. Would Mira do something to him?

Clarissa was frantic. I have to get out of here, she decided. But I can't just stroll out the front entrance.

I need a plan.

She closed the door to her room. Then she went to the window and slid it open.

The lawn was deserted now. A narrow ledge ran along the building, a few feet below her window. A metal drainpipe stood off to her right.

Clarissa slipped on her jacket and climbed out of the second-story window. As she rested a foot on the narrow ledge, she gripped the windowsill and carefully swung her other leg out.

Clarissa took a deep breath. Don't look down, she told herself. She released her hands from the windowsill, and edged toward the pipe. She tried to claw at the building, but there was nothing to hold on to.

At last her free hand touched the drain pipe. She grasped it—hugged it. Clamped her feet on either side.

Her palms squeaked against the metal pipe, the cold quickly turning hot from the friction.

Nice and slow, she told herself.

Then her left foot skidded off the pipe!

She tried to stop herself, but it was no use. Clarissa slid helplessly down the metal pipe.

Gaining speed.

Falling.

Until she hit the ground.

The air whooshed out of her lungs, and sharp pain shot through both ankles.

I'm okay. Get going, she ordered herself.

She tried to stroll casually. She didn't want to attract attention. But after a few seconds she couldn't help herself. She sprinted as fast as she could.

Free. I'm free!

Clarissa slowed down when she approached her house. Exhausted from running so hard, she breathed in deeply through her mouth. She walked up the empty driveway and checked the front door. Locked.

Her parents must still be out shopping. No sign of Mira or Aaron.

She slumped down onto the porch. Now what?

Think, she commanded herself. Use common sense. Who would know where Mira was?

Mira's parents.

Clarissa didn't have any other options. And Mira didn't live far.

She loped down the driveway and didn't look back. In minutes she was ringing the Blocks' bell.

Mrs. Block answered the door. "Clarissa!" she exclaimed. "I'm . . . I'm surprised to see you!"

Clarissa wondered if Mrs. Block knew she was supposed to be at the clinic. If she did, she didn't let on.

"Mrs. Block," Clarissa gasped. "Is Mira around?"

"She's baby-sitting Aaron. Didn't you know?"

"Yeah, I knew," Clarissa said, trying to sound casual. "But I was out for a run and wanted to catch up with them. She mentioned that she might take Aaron for ice cream, but I didn't see them in town."

"I don't know about ice cream," Mrs. Block replied. "But Mira mentioned that she might go to Fear Lake."

Clarissa stiffened. "Fear Lake?"

"Yes. She wanted to rent a boat with Aaron."

"A boat?" Clarissa asked. Her pulse thundered

in her head as she remembered something horrible.

Aaron was terrified of water.

Clarissa scanned the woods around the lake. Her lungs heaved. Her legs wobbled. She had never run so far in her life.

There. In a clearing up ahead she saw Mira's car.

Clarissa had to find her, and fast. She limped toward the water, her sneakers scuffling through the thick carpet of leaves.

She heard a splashing sound.

Her heart rose into her throat as she gazed into the distance.

A small rowboat floated in the middle of the lake.

Aaron was huddled on the bow, while Mira was rocking the boat back and forth. Clarissa could hear Mira laughing.

She had to get out there.

Clarissa scanned the lake for a boathouse, but couldn't find one. She'd have to swim for it.

She raced to the shoreline. "Aaron!" she cried. She dived into the water.

Clarissa gasped as the icy water shocked her skin. She gritted her teeth and swam toward the boat as hard as she could. In seconds her arms and legs were numb.

Pain pierced her chest with every stroke.

Every time Clarissa caught a glance, she saw Mira staring at her from the rowboat. Her backpack on her lap. Calm as can be.

She's waiting for me, Clarissa realized. Maybe she's not really going to hurt Aaron. Maybe I was wrong.

Clarissa treaded water for a moment and locked eyes with Mira.

Mira unzipped the bag. Pulled out Justine's phone. Waved it in the air.

Mira was smiling at her. No. *Laughing* at her.

A sick feeling overcame Clarissa.

She knew. At that moment she knew her best friend was a killer.

"Clarissa!" Aaron called. "Clarissa, I'm scared!"

"Don't worry," Clarissa gasped. "I'm here, Aaron."

"When did they let *you* out?" Mira called.

Clarissa ignored her. "You did it, didn't you? You set Will up. You set us all up!"

"You've finally figured it out?" Mira cried. She grabbed Aaron.

"Which one should I dump first? The phone or the little geek?"

144

Chapter Twenty-three

"Clarissa!" Aaron wailed, standing up. The boat swayed.

"Sit down, Aaron!" Mira snapped. "I mean it!"

Aaron sat, his face pale and meek.

"They might say Aaron's death was an accident," Mira explained. "But I'm pretty sure that they'll blame you for it. You're not exactly *sane*, remember?"

"Mira, don't do this," Clarissa pleaded, churning in the freezing water. "Please—"

"Give it a rest," Mira sneered.

Clarissa's legs burned. She couldn't stay afloat much longer. "Why, Mira?" she cried. "Why are you doing this?"

"You never got it, did you?" Mira said. "Will and I were friends for a *reason*. We were meant to be together. But he only wanted Justine. He was obsessed with her! You read the diary! You know how he was!"

Mira's hand gripped the phone.

"So I had no choice. I had to kill her," she continued, her voice cold and calculated. "I climbed that stupid trellis and pushed her down the stairs." Her face darkened. "But that didn't work, did it?"

"Mira—"

"Shut up!" Mira shrieked. "You ruined everything. I thought Will would want *me* after Justine was gone. But he didn't. He wanted Justine back. And when he couldn't have her, he went for a cheap substitute. You."

Clarissa gulped, trying to stay afloat. Water kept flooding her mouth, but she was too tired to breathe through her nose. She had to do something—fast.

"I was going to kill you," Mira went on. "But then that thing with the psychic started. It made perfect sense. I didn't have to get you out of the way. You were making yourself look crazy without me having to do anything!"

"Drop dead!" Clarissa croaked. Her legs moved weakly. The water splashed up over her chin.

"I didn't want to kill Debra," Mira continued, ignoring her. "But I was stupid. Because I admitted to her one night that I was hot for

Will. And I couldn't give her a chance to figure out that I killed Justine to get her out of the way."

Mira shook her head. "Luckily, she liked to talk on the phone at the top of the stairs as much as Justine. How weird is that?"

Red hot anger shot through Clarissa. But she could hardly stay afloat.

Aaron . . . I've got to get to Aaron, she thought.

Mira let out a loud sigh and plunked the phone into the lake. "Bye-bye, Justine." She waved at the water.

Then she turned to Aaron. "Ready for your swimming lesson?"

Chapter Twenty-four

Clarissa saw a blur of motion.

Then she screamed as her brother's body splashed into the lake.

He sank. He didn't come back up.

Clarissa kicked her legs frantically, thrashing over the water toward him.

"You coward!" she screamed at Mira. "He's only five! He can't swim!"

"That's the point," Mira shot back. "Now Justine has no way to talk to you—or anyone!"

Clarissa dived under, flailing wildly. She had to find Aaron. Had to—

Her hand brushed his shirt.

Clarissa reached out and caught a handful of it. She yanked Aaron close to her and kicked upward.

Aaron struggled.

He was still conscious.

Their heads broke the surface. Clarissa gasped, sucking in the precious air. Aaron coughed and sputtered in her grasp.

"You have to swim," Clarissa choked out.

"I can't!" he wailed.

A sharp stab of pain made Clarissa howl. White lights shot through her vision.

Mira hit her with the oar from the boat!

Clarissa turned in the water. The boat rocked almost on top of them!

Mira lifted the oar for another strike.

Clarissa frantically kicked away from the boat.

Mira grunted and swung the oar at Clarissa's head. But Clarissa threw herself out of the way.

Clarissa knew she couldn't hold out much longer.

"Aaron . . . you're . . . too . . . heavy," she sputtered.

"No, Clarissa!" he cried.

"Take a deep breath," she whispered to Aaron.

The water crept over their heads until darkness surrounded them.

This is it, she thought. She and Aaron were going to drown.

And Mira . . .

Mira could make up any story she wanted.

Aaron drifted away from her grasp.

Clarissa reached out frantically for him.

Got to catch him . . .

She didn't.

Where is he? Clarissa couldn't see anything in the dark, swirling water.

I . . . I can't breathe, Clarissa realized.

Can't hold my breath any longer . . . My chest . . . It's burning . . . burning . . . about to explode.

She plunged up. Broke the surface, splashing, coughing, sucking in air.

Aaron?

Where are you, Aaron?

Don't drown. Oh, please—don't drown.

No sign of him. Nothing. Nothing floating on the bobbing, shimmering lake.

"Noooooooo!" A wail of horror escaped Clarissa's throat.

Not Aaron, too. I couldn't *live* if Aaron died, too.

She spun frantically. Saw Mira rowing toward her. Leaning into it. Coming to finish her off.

And then, splashing sounds . . . toward shore.

With a gasp, Clarissa spun again. And saw a man, fully clothed, swimming hard, kicking away from her.

"I've got the boy!" he called. "Get in the boat—before you drown!"

Who was he? Where did he come from?

Clarissa didn't care. Aaron was safe. Aaron was going to be okay.

Mira paddled to meet her. When she got close enough, she stood up and raised the oar. "I'm sorry, Clarissa!" she cried. "I don't have a choice."

Clarissa clamped her hand on the edge of the boat and pulled down with all her weight.

Mira teetered. The oar spun out of her hand.

Clarissa yanked down again.

Mira let out a screech and flew into the water. She came up quickly.

Clarissa grabbed Mira's head and pushed her under. Then she brought her knee up, into Mira's stomach.

When she let go, Mira dipped beneath the surface. With a desperate cry, Clarissa grabbed the boat. Flipped one leg up over the side.

Her muscles throbbed from the effort, but Clarissa clambered into the boat. She snatched up the second oar and paddled toward shore.

Clarissa looked back. Mira was splashing frantically in the water. Then she began to swim.

Clarissa paddled furiously toward shore. Pain wrenched her body with every stroke.

She glanced behind her and saw Mira, gaining on the boat.

Clarissa paddled harder.

"Whoa—!" She let out a startled cry when she saw her parents and Dr. Sayles standing on the shore.

And several police officers.

She could see an officer helping the man who saved Aaron. They dragged his little body ashore and threw a blanket around him.

He wasn't moving.

Will they believe me now? Clarissa wondered. Will they?

All she could do was pray. . . .

She paddled the rest of the way to shore. Two policemen and her father helped her out of the boat.

"Thank heaven Mrs. Block called us!" her mother cried.

Mira staggered out of the water, pointing at Clarissa. "She tried to kill Aaron! She broke out of the hospital so she could kill him! She said he was a replacement for Justine!"

"No!" Clarissa shouted. "That's not true! You have to believe me! Mira killed Justine and Debra!"

Detective Larson turned to Dr. Sayles. They didn't move. Clarissa's parents shared a look as well.

Oh, no, Clarissa thought. They don't believe me!

"He's dead!" Mira screamed. "Aaron! He's dead!"

Aaron lay stretched out on a blanket, eyes shut, mouth open.

He didn't move.

His face was deathly pale.

His lips an eerie blue.

"He's dead," Mr. Turner moaned. "Aaron is dead."

Chapter Twenty-five

"**N**o!" Clarissa wailed. "He can't be dead!"

"Clarissa," Detective Larson said softly. "Better come with me."

"But I didn't do it!" Clarissa screamed. "I swear I didn't! Mira confessed—"

Clarissa turned helplessly to her parents. Tears streamed down Mrs. Turner's cheeks. Her father stood solemnly over Aaron, a stunned, blank look on his face.

"No!" Clarissa cried, gazing at her little brother. "I didn't—"

She stopped when something caught her eye.

No . . . it couldn't be, she thought.

But it was.

Justine's phone? Yes! It had somehow

washed up to the shore. The shallow murky water rippled gently, holding it afloat.

"Come on," Larson demanded. "Let's get you into some dry clothes and—"

Clarissa heard a cough.

"Aaron!" her father cried.

Aaron coughed again. A geyser of water shot out of his mouth.

An officer lifted him up and pounded his back. Aaron spit up more water.

His eyes fluttered open.

"He's alive!" Clarissa shrieked.

Mira ran to Aaron's side. She stroked his hand. "Are you okay, Aaron? I was so scared!"

Detective Larson let out a sigh. "You're lucky, Clarissa. Let's all go now."

He guided Clarissa toward the patrol car.

Clarissa couldn't believe this was happening to her. No one believes me, she thought hopelessly. And now I'm going back to the clinic—probably forever.

Then she heard something.

A tiny hoarse voice.

At first, Clarissa couldn't make out the words.

"What did you say, Aaron?" Clarissa's father was demanding.

"She did it!" Aaron cried, loud enough for them all to hear. "Mira tried to kill us!"

* * *

The phone on Clarissa's nightstand rang.

Clarissa flipped the antenna up, and hit On. "Hello?"

"It's me," Will said.

"Aren't you supposed to be here already?" Clarissa teased him. She grabbed a tube of lipstick off her dresser.

"Uh . . . yeah. I'm running a little late. I still have a cast on my leg. Slows me down."

"Excuses, excuses," Clarissa replied, chuckling. "Hurry or we're going to be late for Stacy's party."

"I'll be there," he promised. "But you better be ready to go."

"Oh, we'll see." Clarissa laughed.

She set the phone down and gazed into the mirror, remembering the times she would watch her sister getting ready to go out.

Good memories, she told herself.

She and Will had apologized to each other at least a hundred times that week. He still didn't believe her about the psychic. But at least he forgave her for pushing him off the trellis.

They both understood they had a lot of pain to get over.

Mira was gone. In a hospital somewhere, getting the help she needed.

Clarissa's father let her keep Justine's phone. She stared at it now. She kept it on the dresser.

No. She'd never hook it up.
Just in case Justine wanted to reach her . . .
The doorbell rang.
Clarissa checked her smile in the mirror, then hurried down to greet Will.

R.L. Stine
Seniors
a FEAR STREET series

available from Gold Key® Paperbacks